The Masters Review
ten stories

The Masters Review

The Masters Review Volume XII
Stories Selected by Toni Jensen
Edited by Cole Meyer, Brandon Williams, and Jen Dupree

Front cover design by Emelie Mano
Interior design by Kim Winternheimer and Julianne Johnson

ISBN: 979-8-9882557-9-6

© 2024 *The Masters Review*. Published annually by *The Masters Review*. All rights reserved. No part of this publication may be reproduced or reprinted without prior written permission of *The Masters Review*. To contact an author regarding rights and reprint permissions please contact *The Masters Review*. www.mastersreview.com

To receive new fiction, contest deadlines,
and other curated content right to your inbox,
send an email to newsletter@mastersreview.com

The Masters Review
ten stories

Volume XII

Ana Kornblum-Laudi • Katherine Cart
Isabelle Shifrin • Leah Edwards
Daniel Monzingo • Will James Limón
Jenny Hayden Halper • Kristin Burcham
Allison Backous Troy • Dyanne Stempel

Stories Selected by
Toni Jensen

Contents

Introduction • ix

Model Home • 1

Good Daughter • 21

Stillborn • 29

Spider Tim • 45

The Swans • 55

Young Again • 63

An Afternoon at the Edge of the World • 79

Beyond Reproach • 97

Sow • 111

The Wedding Dress • 117

Introduction

When I teach creative writing courses or do editorial work, like judging, for journals and anthologies, I'm often asked what I'm looking for in a short story or an essay. The person presumably seeks an indication of aesthetics, tastes, preferences in subject matter. I've given the matter a fair amount of thought, then, but I return, each time, to a fairly simple answer, one I'm sure makes me seem difficult or mercurial. My answer is: surprise me.

It's my best, genuine response to the question of what draws me to stories, what I value in essays, what moves me the most while reading in any genre, the element of surprise. The stories and essays I've chosen to be included in this year's anthology of *The Masters Review* all do this—offer surprise upon surprise—in language and imagery, in narrative and voice. Each of the ten pieces in this anthology elicits a sense of surprise or wonder, a giggle or gasp. Each tells a complete and riveting story. Each has mastered the art of pushing its characters and language away from the expected or mundane.

Yet life's mundanity is explored in these pieces as often as is the extraordinary. There's a trick to doing this, of course, making common or collectively held experiences both familiar and strange.

All the pieces in this anthology offer us this dual gift of recognition and surprise.

In some of these stories, the elements of surprise are multitiered or layered. In "The Wedding Dress," a bride redefines the rituals of the night before a wedding, and the surprises come through both the language and the plot. In "The Swan," the delicate balancing of the conflict during two teenagers' budding friendship offers a surprise when the plot takes a turn, and the tensions also build throughout the story through the place descriptions and other fine details. "An Afternoon at the Edge of the World" features wonderful strangeness in its location, but the emotional layers of the story offer additional surprises. In "Beyond Reproach," situational conflict provides surprises, but also throughout the story, the decisions of the middle class, middle-aged characters surprise both readers and themselves. "Sow" offers a narrative that uses evocative language alongside the act of growing plants to stand in for so many other complexities of emotion and relationship. "Spider Tim" combines a strong and startling narrative voice and a fascinating setting to move readers toward an unexpected emotional turn.

It's often the emotional turn at the end of a story that provides the largest surprise. In some of these stories, the elements of surprise are woven throughout expertly so that the ending provides the rare pleasure of an inevitable surprise. "Young Again" is one such story, focusing on the relationship between a teenager and his grandfather. "Model Home" is another, providing an unexpected unfolding of an affair. In "Good Daughter," a farmer's daughter cares for ill family members and must decide what kind of life she wants for herself. "Stillborn" puts forward the story of a family working the peppermint fields, and the main character's language at the end of the story is what provides the compelling turn toward surprise.

I enjoyed reading all the submissions for this year's *Masters Review* anthology, so picking these ten was an enjoyable but also difficult task. The ten stories and essays offered here hold a wide range of subject matter and place, characters' voices, and conflict upon conflict. They also all use language impeccably. They will surprise you in all the best ways.

—*Toni Jensen*
Guest Judge

Model Home
Ana Kornblum-Laudi

When I was a kid, I used to imagine what my house looked like from the outside, to someone who didn't live there. I'd start with the smallest details—the chipped red heart my sister drew on the mailbox in glittery nail polish; the tangle of ivy climbing hungrily up the façade, peeling away paint; the mess of limbless Barbie dolls and plastic bicycles strewn around the front lawn. With each detail, I'd work my way inward, closer to the interior. I envisioned different scenes like disjointed frames from a movie reel: My mother and father passing each other wordlessly in the kitchen; my sister sleepwalking down the hallway, ripping the wooden kiddie gate my parents installed at the top of the staircase off its creaking hinges, fleeing into the cool night air in her bunny-print pajamas. My dad in the living room, screaming, throwing objects at walls. My mom perched silently at the foot of the basement stairs, biting the flesh of her hand. The purpled crescents her teeth left after she'd returned smilingly upstairs.

This was my odd little ritual. I don't know why I did it. I guess I was trying to figure something out, to organize the picture.

* * *

I do the same thing now after your husband leaves me and returns to you. I try to imagine what happens when he gets home. I start with the exterior and zoom in: the tidy, unchipped lavender of your Victorian home's façade; the bay windows on the second floor that overlook the street, too high up to see into. When he walks inside, I see your framed wedding poster—something traditionally Quaker about the document, he explained to me once—displayed prominently on a wall in the entryway, your squiggly signatures in the lower left corner. All ugly household objects—tissues, for instance, or thumbtacks—are hidden in beautiful containers around the house. There are rarely dishes in the sink. Maybe he opens the door quietly and peels off his shoes in the foyer. Does he slink upstairs before saying hello? Does he bother to acknowledge your presence at all? Do you try to intervene, or do you keep to yourself, stand stoically at the marble island in the kitchen listening to the stairs creak one by one?

Here is another scenario: You are sitting in the living room with whichever of your adolescent children happen to be around at the time, the two or three of you watching a movie together. Gabriel removes his shoes at the door and breezes into the kitchen to pour himself a glass of water. *What're you watching?* he asks, taking a sip and leaning casually against the marble island. Your small act of defiance is not acknowledging his question. One of your children answers. Then he joins you and the kids on the couch and watches along with you. He does not strike me as the kind of person who would be cautious or considerate enough to shower first. You keep your gaze fixed on the kaleidoscopic blur of the TV screen.

Haven't you ever smelled me on him? Have you asked him about it? Maybe you are tired of asking questions. Perhaps you've asked them too many times already, before me.

* * *

There are questions I want to ask you: On a Tuesday night, do you ever think, *Where is my husband?* Do you know enough to hate me? Maybe you find me pathetic. Perhaps some cool, distanced part of you also finds me pitiable, a sad little creature caught in someone else's web, or an insect that keeps flinging itself dumbly into flame. Or maybe I drive you crazy with paranoia, make you feel like a detective in your own relationship. Mostly, though, I want to know whether you, too, have ever felt afraid of your husband.

* * *

I have started having dreams about you. Nothing happens in them. I just watch you move silently from room to room in your house. No one else is there—not Gabriel, not me, not your kids. All I register is a heavy feeling, some vertiginous swell of sadness and guilt and shame tugging, always, at the ugly, hungry pit of me.

* * *

Sometimes I search for you online. I feel cool and remote in these moments, caught in a tenuous spell of omniscience. I don't know what I hope to find. I glance at articles you've written, skim book reviews. I am not interested in the things that thrill you: the biological mechanisms of memory, neurological illness, addiction. In a video interview Gabriel posted to his Twitter feed, you're sitting in front of a golden pothos plant I gave him. It's placed neatly on the mantel behind you beside a strategically situated copy of the book you've just published, the whole display too symmetrical and deliberate. Watching the video, I'm struck by an impression of unreality—something to do with the inclusion of this dirty secret, this symbol of betrayal, in your nationally televised interview. Often, it's small things like this that shock me most, awaken me to the casual violence of what I'm doing.

In the video, you speak beautifully.

I click through the same three photos of you. I recognize where one of them was taken: in front of the narrow stream a few blocks from your house. Once, I gave Gabriel a blowjob there in broad daylight, in the exact spot you're standing in. I was astounded by our recklessness even as it was happening. Afterwards, he told me he loved me. I said I really cared about him too. He didn't seem to mind. He picked me up and lay us both down a few steps away at the foot of that tree that leans precariously over the edge of the water. I don't remember what we were talking about except that it had to do with the time I reported my high school English teacher for sleeping with one of my peers, a shy girl named Alexis. I was terrified throughout the process, disinclined as I was to challenging others, though I spoke frankly with administrators and the police, even after my English teacher's pleas had turned to harassment and threats. *You're brave, you know that?* Gabriel had said, brushing a strand of hair out of my eyes. *There's nothing in-your-face about it, though. It's a kind of quiet pluck I really admire. You're not un-anxious, but you've always done what feels right to you.* Something about this expression of familiarity and knowing warmed me; made me feel, for an instant, like I wasn't any plaything he'd chosen at random. I was struck by how perfect a description it was of the person I used to be, before all of this began, and by how well he'd known me then.

Over and over again, despite myself, I slip into an old, easy warmth for him. That night, I'd gone home soothed by the smell of him on me. For what felt like a shamefully long time, I lolled about in bed with my shirt pressed to my face, breathing him in. Then I stood up, peeled off my clothes, and scalded myself in the shower. I used too much soap, scrubbed my skin raw.

I close my browser when the memory surfaces, a familiar horror creeping up on me. Then I go for a two-mile sprint along the river until my lungs reject air.

* * *

My roommate, Sasha, is a fan of your work. She first encountered it when she cyberstalked you once while I lay on the couch in our living room with my head in her lap, talking in circles about your husband. "This woman's brilliant," she said. It's true.

Sasha works in a wet lab that performs behavioral experiments on rats. She gets them hooked on cocaine and observes them as they devolve into obsessive, lever-pressing addicts. *My little hungry ghosts*, she calls them.

I visited her at work the other day after parting ways with Gabriel in a hotel parking lot, waltzed right into her lab with blurred makeup and sex hair. Sasha was wearing her lab coat and delicately handed me a hair tie so I wouldn't contaminate her samples as I trailed her from room to room.

"You know who he reminds me of?" she said.

"Who?"

"My dad."

Sasha's father is a notorious Ukrainian con artist. He owned a medical equipment production company in Kyiv before he was arrested on charges ranging from fraud and embezzlement to close professional affiliations with prominent cartels and human trafficking rings.

"If my dad meditated and hung out with Oprah and pretended to be a good person."

I laughed for a second, but quickly, I didn't find it funny anymore and stopped. In one of my imaginary frames, I picture Gabriel hiding your keys to make you think you're losing your mind. I watch you sprint feverishly around the living room overturning pillows, digging through laundry bins, crawling under tables. Gabriel pretends to help.

"And you know who you remind me of?" Sasha said, gesturing toward the animals, her little hungry ghosts. "All day long: *tap, tap, tap*." She mimed each *tap* with her index finger. "They go crazy after a while."

Briefly, I took stock of all the things I was too confused by, or ashamed of, to tell Sasha. *What is happening to me?* I wanted to ask her. *Why can't I leave him?* Then I dragged my fingernails punishingly along the skin of my bare thighs. *You're an adult*, I silently chastised myself. *Stop making excuses for yourself.* I watched a white lab rat with a wire protruding from its skull press its nose quaveringly against the glass pane of its enclosure before darting into a cardboard shoebox.

* * *

Because of your husband, I have Googled insane things. *Is it normal to fantasize about your spouse dying?* (Apparently, it is.) He told me once that you mentioned you'd lost weight and he had registered the hopeful thought, *I wonder if it's malignancy.*

"I would of course never wish that on anyone," he clarified laughingly. "But everyone would be so understanding," he said, if you were to simply die. "There would be no blame, no accusations." His life could move seamlessly forward without you.

Again, an image of you wandering from room to room in your house, paired with a queasy heaviness, a whisper of shame.

He was talking about feeling trapped in your marriage and planning to leave you to run away with me. "I have all these totally unsexy fantasies about it," he said. "Me cleaning our apartment while you're at work; us reading together on the couch. I want to argue with you. I want to pull your hair out of the shower drain each morning. There's still so much I want to experience with you."

I'd smiled at him with a sinking feeling and had the terrible thought, *This will never end.* He has never asked me if *I* want him to run away with me, though I haven't managed to tell him outright that that isn't what I want. I am afraid of him, and I am afraid of what he'll do if I leave him, and I'm afraid of losing him altogether. I don't know anymore what it is I am trying to let go of.

"What do you think her experience of the relationship is?" I asked him gently.

"Huh," he said, tilting his head to one side as if this consideration had never occurred to him. "That's a good question." He looked up at the sky. "I think she's happy."

I tried to discern whether he actually believed this or if he was just saying it. "Have you two ever talked about it?"

"No. She wouldn't be open to those kinds of discussions. She cares about the façade of marriage, and from the outside, we look like the perfect couple."

Often, I think that every judgment your husband makes about you reflects a quality he rejects in himself. He would never have a conversation like that, for example—he cannot tolerate criticism or constructive feedback, anything that threatens his flimsy impression of himself as just shy of omnipotent—and I have never met someone more concerned with appearances. I don't know you well enough to say whether you suffer the same affliction.

What was it like with you at the beginning? I asked him. He said that you were the kindest person he'd ever met, that he felt very comfortable with you.

"I've always been grateful to her for that. But it's been twenty-five years. How long do I have to feel grateful for? She doesn't really see me. I mean, in certain ways, she knows me well. But we're very different people. That loneliness that will always be there. And even at the beginning, it wasn't love."

Again, he looked up at the sky. "Well—" he said, and stopped. He lowered his eyebrows thoughtfully. "I—I don't—Well, I guess that was love."

Watching him swim in his private confusion, I thought, *This man has no idea what love feels like.* I registered a familiar swell in my chest, an impulse to hug his creepy void-self and make it feel okay.

It is not uncommon to catch your husband in an unwitting expression of vulnerability like this, and I have come to feel protective of him in these moments, careful to not embarrass him. He lives his life defensively, like he expects everyone to harm him if given half a chance, and I want him to feel safe with me. I willed my face into dumb neutrality and nodded, thinking about how hollow a life like his must feel, one that is not loveless in a pedestrian sense, but rather insofar as he seems somehow constitutionally incapable of love. *Something is wrong with him*, I thought. *It isn't his fault he is the way he is.*

I reached out to brush a fruit fly off his cheek, and before I pulled my hand away, he took it in his and held my palm flat against the side of his face, smiling softly and letting his eyes slide shut. The tenderness of the gesture made me want to weep.

I focused on the fruit fly, which migrated through the air in slow circles before resettling on his collarbone.

There is something tragic about your husband, isn't there? He's a stranger in the truest sense of the term, unknowable to himself and others. Beneath his thin façade of confidence and grandiosity, he is only ever one small step away from a bottomless well of shame, and he doesn't know how to be close with anyone unless he's controlling them. Often, I think that he's the loneliest person I know; that his whole life is a house of cards built around proving to himself and the world that he's good, significant, worthy. That he isn't a monster.

Other times, I think I've gotten it all wrong—that perhaps all your husband cares about is power. Months ago, when I applied for jobs around the country, he reached out to acquaintances he had in the music world, high-profile composers and conservatory directors, and passed along my name and contact information without asking my permission. When I considered moving to Oregon for a teaching position, he tried to persuade your son to apply to college at the university I'd be working within. And all this year, he has been offering me money, though he has never specified what it is he believes I need financial help with. *Just think about it*, he says when I decline. He texts me the same link to a cryptocurrency site. *I care about you. I would help out any of my loved ones like this.* Increasingly, the care your husband feels for the people he claims to love reminds me of the cool, abstracted empathy humans feel for the animals we consume as meat.

* * *

Is it normal to tell your mistress that you fantasize about your spouse dying?
Does my partner have NPD?
Stages of grooming

* * *

Have there been others like me, pretty young things your husband invites into your home and parades around your neighborhood?

Gabriel Velasco sexual harassment allegations
Gabriel Velasco civil suits
Gabriel Velasco malpractice

* * *

What I find are headlines like *International Expert in Women's Psychiatry Discusses the Enduring Effects of Sexual Abuse*, or *Johns Hopkins Psychologist Talks Bestselling Book on Trauma. Doctor Gabriel Velasco Recommends Mindfulness Practices for Survivors of Sexual Assault. Gabriel Velasco, PhD Joins Board of Directors at Oprah Winfrey's Organization for Young Women.* All of it reinforces my suspicion that I've lost my mind. Perhaps, I think, again and again, he is just a normal guy who fell in love with the wrong person at the wrong time. There is no way he would be who he is if this were not the case. I read and reread interviews, dissect clips of your husband's TV appearances, testing the theory. In the videos, he speaks with a warmth and softness I remember being charmed by when I first met him. Now, it startles and confuses me, the ease with which he slips into this other self.

Your husband, the globally renowned psychologist. He is famous in a field that doesn't typically produce celebrities. He's an expert in trauma disorders and sexual abuse, the founder of the world's foremost treatment facility for young women with such afflictions, a darling among the A-list Hollywood celebrities and high-profile politicians he works with who moonlight as mental health advocates. He is known for taking on the most hopeless cases, the untouchables of the psychiatric community: the chronically suicidal; the so-called cluster Bs; the patients every other therapist has rejected.

You are your husband's second wife. His first wife was also his first psychiatric patient. That was thirty years ago, when he treated her after she'd admitted to the ICU in the wake of a near-lethal suicide attempt. She'd swallowed a bottle of pills after her boyfriend broke up with her and spent the following week in a coma. He began dating her immediately after she discharged from the hospital, and within months, they were married. Not two years in, he left her.

He has written a memoir about the relationship, which he promotes online and at national psychiatric conferences. Do you not find the book disturbing? In the opening pages, Gabriel talks about how, even with tubes protruding from every orifice in her body and a plastic sack of her excrement dangling off the side of her hospital bed, his patient had seduced him. He talks about how stunning and vibrant she was, how vertiginous his infatuation. There is so much sex that half the book reads like soft-core erotica. The narrator is patently misogynistic and lacking in self-awareness. He sees nothing wrong with his behavior. *After all*, he reasons when he transfers his love interest to a locked psychiatric unit, *she was no longer my patient.* Reading it was the first time I remember feeling repulsed by him.

He remains bafflingly obsessed with his first wife, doesn't he? Haunted, even. Rarely a week slides by in which he does not mention her, though he has never described his lingering fixation in a way that makes sense. *No one has made me feel more loved* is all he ever says. Still, she is the reason he devoted the rest of his life to treating young women with trauma disorders. I think about that a lot.

The book is dedicated to you. It received rave reviews from the nation's other foremost psychiatric professionals, his colleagues. He hands out copies to his coworkers and patients. You were its editor. Over and over again, I decide I must be missing something.

* * *

When I first became your husband's patient, he was the only person who knew me well, and back then, before his interest assumed the thinness of obsession, I never doubted how much he cared for me. I suppose this is what I am trying to let go of.

That was five years ago, when your husband did a semester of pro bono counseling at my university following a string of student suicides. For as long as I could remember, I had been plagued by an apparently sourceless despair, and that autumn, all I thought about was death. I'd begun squirreling away pills from my mother's medicine cabinet, and when I walked across the bridge to go to class each morning, I'd pause and press my body against the railing, testing myself. In the evenings, I wandered around my neighborhood in wide, idle loops, marveling at the life unfolding all around me—parents playing catch with their kids; couples walking hand in hand—and feeling like an alien, envious at this easy display of normalcy.

Quickly, I became your husband's favorite. "I don't normally do this," he said when, a few weeks in, he gave me his cellphone number and encouraged me to call him between sessions. "But I worry about you. I don't want you to feel alone with this." He began scheduling me for multiple appointments each week, even though my insurance only covered four sessions per month; he never asked me to pay for the extra meetings. Sometimes, he'd text me spontaneously. It was small things, mostly, that indicated to me that I was on his mind: a line from a poem he thought I'd like; a photograph of the flowers in your garden. He'd ask me to bring my guitar to session and play him the songs I'd written because, I think, he knew that it mattered to me more than I let on, and eventually, he began offering me projects. To this day, if you visit your husband's website, you can hear me playing airy instrumentals in the background. Occasionally, he'd post my recordings anonymously to his heavily trafficked social media accounts. *Shared by a brilliant young artist*, he'd write. Or: *Thank you to this incomparably talented young woman for reminding me why I do what I do.*

After his pro bono term ended, your husband began inviting me over to your house for coffee or dinner with you and the kids. I have spent slow-moving Sundays curled up on your couch, chatting with your family. In those days, your husband felt like a father to me, and I registered a shameful, fugitive longing to be absorbed into his life, wanting it to ground me. (It is true what he used to say: I have always been a little hungry for love.) I imagined joining your family on your annual trips to Martha's Vineyard, the five of us splayed out on beach towels reading together in easy silence. You seemed so unlike my own family, who had never had a peaceful Sunday evening together or a weekend getaway that did not end in violence, and we certainly did not gather in the living room simply to enjoy one another's company. Your husband knew that I avoided going back to my parents' during school breaks, and when the other students left campus and migrated home for the holidays, he picked me up in the city and drove me to your house so that I wouldn't be alone.

I was unaccustomed to feeling special to someone. Back then, your husband was the only person I didn't seem to frighten or disturb; the only one who knew how damaged I was and still wanted me around. If you had asked me years ago, I'd have said that he saved my life. Still, despite everything, I often think it's true.

Eventually, he began telling me he loved me, but it would be like this: *I love you, kiddo*, with a clap on the back if I said something funny or insightful. Or: *I feel very connected to you. I don't have that with many people. These days, I only spend time with the friends I really love.* Then he'd do something that confused me, like pull me in for a long, intimate hug or reach over to tuck an errant strand of hair behind my ear, holding my gaze and smiling wistfully at me. Or he'd say: *I've never had nor wanted a friendship with someone half my age. But with you, I don't notice the age gap. There's something romantic about our relationship, isn't there? I find myself wanting to spend the whole day with you, the whole night with you.* If I withdrew and said, *We should be careful*, he'd tell me that I'd misunderstood him; he had been talking about emotional intimacy, not physical. He had simply been noting these thoughts aloud in the interest of full transparency. Occasionally, he acknowledged, our closeness confused him. He was very sorry if anything he'd said had made me uncomfortable.

"You know that even if I did have feelings for you, I would never in a million years act on them. Right?"

"Why else would you say anything?" I'd reply with a disarming smile, privately hurt and humiliated and angry. I was also deeply, unmistakably flattered. I have always felt that way with your husband: at once chosen and utterly dispensable.

"God," he'd say earnestly, pressing the palm of his hand to his heart. "I would never. That would be universally destructive. I wish you knew how much I care about you."

Afterwards, he'd disappear. For days or weeks at a time, I'd hear nothing from him. He stopped calling during his lunch breaks or on the commute home from work. He turned on his read receipts and left my messages unanswered. It was in his absence that I registered how dependent on him I'd become. I missed him so much I half believed I'd fallen a little in love with him, and I felt what I'd always imagined physical withdrawals might feel like: a queasy panic, an animal need. I became obsessed with getting his attention back; with figuring out what had changed and why. I wanted him to prove something to me. I am still waiting for him to prove it.

Eventually, he'd reach out as if nothing had happened, and I'd be so relieved I wouldn't ask for an explanation. I never forgot the lesson, though. Here is something I would never say aloud: Often, it occurs to me that one of the reasons I let this begin in the first place is that I didn't want to confirm what I think I already know—that the second I am no longer useful to your husband, he will discard me.

* * *

For a while, I was doing well. I was excelling in school, winning contests for the compositions your husband encouraged me to submit. I had close friends and a kind, unproblematic boyfriend. Your husband had been my therapist for a year by then, and it was the first time in my life that I remember feeling not just normal, like the ground wouldn't slip out from under me at any moment, but content.

I suppose I am still doing well, relatively speaking. These days, though, I feel fragile again, like I did when I first met your husband.

I know that he's part of the problem, that something about what we're doing is making me unravel. But often, I suspect that he's also the only thing keeping me intact. After all, I have never been all right without him. Now, when I do something wrong and he withdraws, I come a little undone. I stay in bed for days on end, call out of work, stop eating, almost catatonically depressed and panicked at the prospect of losing him. Sometimes, I slice up my forearms or thighs just to get out of the spin of my head.

I lie about it all to Sasha, my sole witness, tell her I'm feeling ill again. But Sasha is not naïve. "I don't get it," she said the other day, sprinting around my bedroom pulling curtains back from windows. "What is this fucking spell he has you under?" She sounded angry when she said it, or exasperated, but she looked scared. I didn't know how to answer her question, so I rolled over in bed to face the wall and said nothing, feeling ashamed and utterly alone. "This isn't an affair, okay? It's sexual abuse," she continued, her voice still tinny with hysteria. "And I don't know how to help you anymore." I kept my body still and silent and turned from her until I heard the swish of her pant legs as she exited my room. Then I bit down on the skin of my hand to keep myself from sobbing. I know that it's wrong, what your husband is doing with me; but he's the only person in the world I want to tell about it.

* * *

Once, years ago, when I was having dinner at your house, your husband touched your shoulder spontaneously and I saw you flinch. It was not the common recoiling of a spouse who finds their partner's touch repellant, or the physical discomfort of two people who have not had sex in a very long time. Rather, you seemed suddenly afraid of him. In the instant after it happened, you glanced at me, and I understood that I'd witnessed something I wasn't supposed to see. I became very interested in my linguini. I laughed at whatever it was your husband had been saying. Then the landscape of your face reconfigured itself into a tranquil smile. You reached across the table and took your husband's hand in yours, kissing its upturned palm, something about the gesture rigid and theatrical. It was the only time I'd ever seen the two of you touch.

I've thought about it a lot since then, the flinch. What was it you had been afraid of? Often, I suspect that your husband is more dangerous than I've been giving him credit for. There are things only you would believe. On two occasions, when I've tried to end the relationship, your husband has threatened to show up at my house unannounced. He says it lightly, with an unreadable smile. *Just a thought experiment: what would you do if I were to just show up at your apartment one night?* It is impossible to know what, exactly, he's threatening, and I am never sure how seriously I should take him. Still, I shut up when he says it, gripped by an animal anxiety. My behavior becomes primitive in these moments, apologetic, every fiber of my being singularly focused on placating him.

Once, after the third and final time I suggested we end our romantic involvement, your husband told me a story about his closest friend, a retired FBI agent and the only person he's mentioned me to, who could track anyone without their knowing. He'd been driving me home at the time and we were stopped at a red light. Suddenly, he pressed down on the gas pedal and sped through it, accelerating to eighty miles per hour, ninety, ninety-five. We flew through stop signs and school zones and residential neighborhoods. All the while, he spoke calmly. For a particular job, he said, the friend had hacked a woman's phone and gained access to her camera; for months, he watched her go about her life from the comfort of his living room in Park Slope. "She liked singing to herself while she cooked and cleaned," he added.

Days earlier, I'd joked with your husband about how I sing soulful classics while cooking myself dinner or cleaning my apartment. I sent him a video Sasha had made of me belting out "Feeling Good" while sauteing vegetables in our sad little kitchen. Our A/C unit had broken that morning and I was wearing only underwear and a sports bra, my body slick with sweat. I held up a spatula as if it were a microphone. In the background, Sasha is laughing.

Please slow down was all I could say. Then he slowed to a crawl and dialed the friend's number. He put the call on speaker phone so that I could hear the conversation. "I'm sitting with her now," he said to the man, not meeting my gaze. "She's wearing very little clothing." I watched him dumbly for a moment, waiting for something: an indication of remorse; an apology for having made a bad joke. "I was just telling her about your job," he continued instead, and for the following fifteen minutes, I made small talk with the stranger's disembodied voice.

That day in the lab, I'd been trying to tell Sasha something, but the words wouldn't knit themselves together. Something is wrong with my perception lately. Memories disappear only to resurface in moments of panic, and I've become so paranoid that it's hard to tell what's real. Even as the thought materialized, I could feel it disintegrating, and already I'd begun to doubt my impression of the interaction I'd had with Gabriel earlier that evening. It was entirely possible, I thought, then and now, that I'd misunderstood him.

We'd been lying in a hotel bed with our limbs entangled, listening to the purr of traffic outside. Something about the moment—the smell of him all over me; the rush of hormones; the knowledge that soon, he'd stand up and collect his clothing from around the floor, locate his keys, leave to make it home in time for dinner—overwhelmed me, and I'd had an impulse to hug him and not let go. I reached for his hand and ran an index finger chastely over the ridges of knuckles and tendons, the cool gold of his wedding band, noticing the age spots on his skin and registering, with a pang, that he was approaching the final stretch of his life.

"What?" he laughed warmly, rolling over on his side to face me. "You look pensive."

"No. Just neurotic, as usual."

"What're you thinking about?"

"How you won't always be around."

He let out a startled laugh. "Pipe down, kid. I've got a few years left."

"I'll stop talking about your mortality. I don't want you to have a heart attack." I tried to say it lightly, shifting the mood I'd set into motion, but I felt an inarticulable sadness showing. It occurred to me—sharply, as it does on occasion—that all this time, I'd been trying to find a way back to a beginning that wasn't real. In his nakedness, he appeared fragile, and it was hard to believe that I'd ever felt afraid of him. *He is sick*, I thought, too, *and he never left you when you were ill.* I have a suspicion I can't explain that if the edifice of your husband's life were to shatter in a particular way—if his public persona were compromised, for instance, his delusions ruptured beyond repair—he would kill himself. This fear is never far from the forefront of my mind.

He smiled at me softly then, pulling the bedsheet up to cover my torso and breasts. "I love you, you know that?" he said, reaching over to touch my cheek. "You're the one good thing I have."

All at once, he looked nervous, or embarrassed, tapping his free hand on the headboard. A few moments elapsed before he added, "Would you tell me if this was hurting you?"

I knew how I was supposed to respond. I was supposed to say something that would reassure him: He had done nothing wrong; I was not going to leave him. Your husband is lethally afraid of criticism, rejection, abandonment. It is important to make him feel wanted, to let him feel like he is always in control. Still, I heard myself say, "I think this is hurting me." I was aware of appealing, recklessly, to some care and humanity I knew I felt once—to whatever it was, perhaps, that had made his nervous tapping begin.

He flashed me a sad smile, withdrawing his hand, and I knew that I'd made a mistake. He did not acknowledge my comment. Instead, out of nowhere, he began talking about one of his patients, a man who'd left his wife to marry his much-younger mistress. "He was always telling me, *It's the happiest I've ever been. I've never loved someone like I love her.* I kept thinking of you, because it reminded me of how I feel now, with you."

As he continued, though, I found I couldn't follow the story. The timeline kept shifting; details changed from one moment to the next. At first, your husband said that he'd begun seeing both the man and his wife for couple's therapy, but minutes later, he claimed that he was initially only treating the husband. He had begun seeing them recently, he told me, but later, he implied that he'd known the man for years ("He was young when I met him," your husband said). It occurred to me that I'd lost my mind, or he was trying to confuse me. The wife was stunning, he kept adding, and I understood that he wanted me to feel jealous. That he was punishing me for something.

"The man had been seeing this hot shot psychologist for fifteen years. He was always very impressed by how intuitive the therapist was, how he seemed to just know things about the man's life without him having to say very much. Recently, however, the man discovered that his wife had secretly started seeing the same therapist herself after he'd brought her to one of his sessions years ago. The therapist had taken her on as a patient, in other words. So, of course, she'd been feeding him this information all along. He discovered, too, that for the decade the therapist had been treating the wife without the husband's knowledge, she and the therapist had been having an affair. (She had always had a thing for male authority figures.) The man had never missed a single appointment, not even when he went on vacation. He found out this week, though, and it was the first time he didn't show up."

I was silent while your husband spoke, registering an incipient panic rising in me. He told the story calmly, without affect, as if he were commenting on the weather. He expressed no empathy for the couple whose lives had been systematically dismantled. *What is wrong with the therapist?* I didn't dare ask. *Why are you telling me this?* I considered your husband's threats, the psychologist's satanic God complex. It occurred to me that if your husband was capable of calculatedly destroying people's lives like this with no remorse—if he were the kind of person who would confess to doing so and get off on watching me squirm—then I didn't know him at all. It was the impression of being suddenly in the company of a stranger that frightened me most. He could be the kind of person who would rape me right there in the hotel room if he got mad enough, or the kind of person who would stalk me for the rest of my life if I left him.

I couldn't discern how realistic the fear was, but instinctively—apologetically—I kissed him. No awareness preceded the action, and I was startled to find my body in motion, as if my attention were elsewhere, somewhere above me. All I could focus on was keeping the bad thing, whatever it was, from happening.

Your husband laughed, not altogether unkindly, turning to face me again. "What made you do that?" he asked. His expression wasn't unsmiling, but there was a manic edge to it that made me nervous. Unsure of how to respond, I shrugged like a child, feeling suddenly ashamed, as if I were leading him on without really meaning to.

"I was prepared to never touch you again," he said, reaching under the bedsheet to slip a hand between my thighs, "but you need to not tempt me." Silently, I let him kiss my neck, my breasts. I let him choke me and enter me without a condom. I faked a very theatrical orgasm, wanting to make it stop. All I thought with any clarity was, *Don't flinch.*

* * *

Here is a question: Do you ever feel as though you're looking at your life from the outside, like a stranger? I do not like the ugly thing I've become. If you were to ask me, I would say, defensively, *This is not me. This is not who I am*, and part of me would believe it. But more and more, I see traces of your husband in me, the way I toy with your life.

I do not envy you. I do not want your husband, not like this. The truth is that I pity you. You are the one who is really trapped. You, who have already given your life to this man. Still, sometimes I imagine the three of us carrying on like this forever, you and I orbiting each other in the overlapping space of our lives with your husband, the only two he can seem to keep for very long. The fools who pity and fear him enough to stick around. I will give up my plans to leave the city, whatever it was I used to want, rent a small one-bedroom where your husband will visit me in the evenings on his way home from work. One by one, I will watch my friends get married and have kids. When your husband grows old and infirm, I will sneak into the hospital to visit him when he goes in for cancer treatments, kidney stones, heart attacks; I will cradle him in twin-sized industrial beds. Eventually, when he realizes that I cannot save or distract him from his strange, relentless misery, he will grow tired of me as he has grown tired of you, and in the intervening years, perhaps there will be others. We will sense them at the periphery of our lives like you must sense me now.

ANA KORNBLUM-LAUDI *is an MFA student at the University of Michigan's Helen Zell Writers' Program. Prior to her MFA career, she worked in clinical psychology. She currently lives in Ann Arbor. She can be reached at aklaudi@umich.edu.*

Good Daughter
Katherine Cart

The three chickens, O. thinks, have gone skinnier in the heat. She will get up soon from the porch and close them in the henhouse. Certainly, they are ready to rest. The evening, though darker now, is hot and thick with small things living through summer. The chickens have long been congregating inside the coop. In sundowns, they are like old folks, surprised to be suddenly tired, walking where they have always walked. They have long quit pecking for slow beetles.

O. has always been a good daughter. Her parents told her, early on, that they had not conceived her with this sort of thing in mind. *Really*, they laughed, when they still laughed, *who could plan that far ahead?* They said that they wanted her to *go off*. That it was important that she should be gone from the quiet for a while. They smiled. *But you're a good daughter, you'll visit us.*

She is a good daughter and does not mind not yet being gone.

Or, the chickens are like new toddlers, who decide it is not yet the age to walk and so lay down to sleep on the floor, still with the soft skin of infants.

* * *

Sickness, in the beginning, was nothing but a difference in time. At first, her mother had only begun to sit for too long, often in the kitchen, a little chore gone undone. The faucet running and her mother watching it. The door in early spring open and the cold spilling across the tile, above the base of the cabinets, across her mother's feet, her mother letting the wet come and the heat go. Rice boiled on the stove until it was a black brick, a pot of flame. Time stretched for the ill.

O. had shut off the faucet and closed the door and cut the flame many times. She had brought her mother to bed often and then once, in late July, for the last time. At first, her mother had said, *I'll be up soon.* Then she turned her head to the wall and closed her eyes. Later, she had opened them and searched for her daughter in the dark. When her daughter came she had cried, *I'm thi-i-i-irsty*, frightened as a child.

O. and her parents live in the house far beyond the edge of town.

No, this is not living. Her parents should have died last winter, when it was cold. A few of the chickens died then. She did not tell them, until they asked.

We can only hear the silkies, the three, they said, from their sick beds. In illness, they loved each other again, and spoke once more in the plural.

That was the soup, O. said. *You liked it.*

She told them that she was sorry.

The next day, they turned their heads to her. *It's all right,* they said. *It was good soup. We did like it.*

Now it is very hot, half a year has gone by, and her parents go on being. She looks more like both of them. Or, they look more like her. Her father's face is fleshed with new liquid. Her mother is bony. Her eyes are large and their lids purple. O. does not like to see herself emerge from them.

The porch is silent. Last autumn's rakes still rest in the far corner, the wood of their handles drying in the high heat. The heat is a visitor that will not go. A rash of crows takes flight up out of the hot trees, as though there has been, somewhere O. cannot see, a small and violent act. The forest is, after all, a living thing.

* * *

There was a year when her mother took care of her father. Sickness then was a presence that felt fleeting. It might get up and walk away at any moment, and though it would leave them tired, they would one day forget it had come. O. was eighteen. Invitations to new lives way away out of that town came in the mail, some with scholarships. She put on a purple gown and danced to Outkast. She kissed somebody and was bored by it. She was so disappointed by this boredom. She had thought the kiss would do something to her. She watched a friend fall in love in June and was saddened by all the happiness. The jubilant hickies. The house was a quiet, nailed box. It smelled only of her father's skin. When O. left to go anywhere, she would hose herself down with *eau de toilette* from her mother's vanity.

You aren't smoking, her mother once had said. She had sat like sticks on the porch bench. When O. did not answer, when she paused half-turned on the steps heading out into the world of the little town, and the silence was buzzing, her mother had shaken her head very slowly, as if to keep from tearing anything, as if what kept her neck strong was gone, had gone soft in the night.

No. I get it, her mother said, *no. I do.*

It has been a year, and O. has begun to say to herself as she stands above their beds, *You know, it's really true that people are often paid to do this work. It just really is.*

* * *

The trees are full of the webs of moths, and so a few branches are leafless. They are becoming other things. The moths are doing very well. The vegetable garden O.'s mother once kept is producing hardy grasses. The lettuces have bolted and the mint in the morning releases the dew it's caught and the whole yard smells of it. Inside, her parents cannot smell the mint, nor the dryness of the rake handles. She should open the windows for them, but the bugs would come in, and she is afraid to see where the flies might go. She is afraid they will come too soon.

Because it is Monday, her hands smell of infant's soap. She has sponge-bathed her mother. Tomorrow she will sponge-bathe her father. She will check him for sores. Because it is evening and still too hot, she has held up their skulls tethered on their limp necks and fed them water with a turkey baster. They have closed their eyes in thanks.

The road past the house is red dirt and there has been no rain, so the dirt has turned everything soft. Sometimes trucks go by, like a piece of something tossed into orbit. Usually they do not. She thinks of how her science teacher in high school said once that nothing really touches. It was unbelievable, at the time. Sitting on the porch step, she wipes a finger along her leg, and this too is soft with road dust. She thinks of how she does not touch the dirt she rolls between her fingers. She does not touch the hen's warm eggs, nor the hay and dried mucus she picks from them. She does not touch the skin of her parents. This thought is of great comfort to her, and so she believes it. She thinks it again. Something she didn't know was tight within her throat relaxes. Besides her parents, O. is alone, and like anybody alone, she believes that what she thinks is very large.

A slim, red fox stands at the edge of the yard, where the forest rears from grass. She watches the chickens and then looks towards the young woman seated on the porch steps.

O. believes there is some greater truth beyond the not-touching, that floats there, just out of reach. Perhaps, she sometimes thinks, I am supposed to go to it. It won't come to me. She thinks of how it would be to take the car and not come back. As she often does, she tests this thought for how it feels, pressed against herself. It feels like nothing. It feels like the bone she will hurt in her hand on the chickens that she will not notice until, in later years, it begins to ache. A dry wind comes through the trees, and a songbird cries as though frustrated.

In the yard, the three chickens are sleepy. They are ready to roost. It is a hot, blue night and the galaxies are coming out behind pollen, and the light of stars is falling on the window of her parents. Perhaps they can turn their heads to see it, but she thinks the gutter might be in the way. Later, when the house is empty and rain comes, the gutter will catch the red dirt of the road, the yellow pollen and the fragments of the black shingle. The water will fall into a barrel and the sound will drum in the yard. Many mosquitos will come to stand on the water's surface and lay their eggs.

In the house, it is quiet.

It takes the red fox no time at all to cross the yard. The wings of the hen she steals beat very fast and sound like a wet sheet pulled tight on the line by a high wind. On the porch, O. stands to see into the dusk. The two silkies remaining squawk and take short wing to the henhouse roof.

And now the caught hen begins to cry. It is the sound of dying. The wings' ligaments continue to beat the feathers into the dry earth, and the hen continues to cry and on the roof the two others cluck as though they are annoyed by loss. O. stands very still on the porch steps. The time when she might have stopped this thing from becoming what it is has long passed.

When it is done, and the fox has carried the hen's body a little ways into the woods, the yard is hushed. The house is like a cupped ear. The wind has not stopped moving through the moth webs and the dry and leafless twigs. O. steps off the porch and crosses the yard on which she once crawled in infancy. When she is inside the coop she closes the gate. The two hens left on the hen house roof know her and do not run. They make soft noises within their feathered chests. She reaches out through the hot night and takes one into her arms and finds its neck, she twists it.

It is far more difficult than she thought it would be. The feathers are dry and slippery. The hen struggles. Feathers soft with dirt. The hen struggles and the neck, as she thought it would, does not give. There is popping like knuckles but still the hen kicks. She crouches with the hen in her arms like an infant, but held so tightly. The claws scrape air and it occurs to O. that each foot seeks the skin of her arm, that this is no longer her silkie, but a bird who will fight. She presses the hen against the ground and the wings beat the dust into her face. The light of the moon catches the wet of the eye. With her hands feeling the bone and the air within the bone and between the bone, feeling the softness of the breast meat, she pulls her knee through her arms, brings her foot forward and places this foot on the neck of the hen. Holding the body she stands quickly. She almost falls over. But the neck is suddenly so easy to tear, it gives before she falls, and though in the dark she cannot see the blood, it wets her sock, runs into her sneaker, gathers beneath her instep. The body still kicks. She thinks of a toy she once had, perhaps a doll.

It was a doll, though it had no face. It was the silhouette of a child stitched in cloth and she had lost it somewhere, hadn't she? The dead hen is fighting hard. Her mother had been so frightened that she would miss the doll. Her mother had said, *Look what you've done now,* and twisted a pinch of her back skin until two silent half moons broke there, but they had not searched the store shelves for the doll, they had gone home, her mother not speaking for the whole drive down the roads that turned to dirt, and though O. will not remember this memory long enough to notice it, or the feelings that have come up beside it, she worries that the body of the bird misses its head. That this missing would be incurable. Would be an unknowable grief. This passes through her. The fear of being the cause of something so large gets in her heart, skips it, and then is gone. She drops the hen's head into the dust.

The second hen has fled into the coop's corner. But the hen knows her and does not run. O. takes this hen by the legs, raises it above her head, and beats it once on the ground. She kills this one in the same way as the first, and it is also quicker than she expected.

* * *

Inside the house it is hot and still. She takes the keys from the counter and fills two bottles with water. The water runs over her hands, and feathers she didn't know were stuck are washed into the sink. She does not turn on the light but can feel the blood, how it sticks in the webbing of her fingers. How it will be there browning when the sun comes. She finds her mother's wallet and stands still in the dark kitchen for a moment.

It's all right! O. calls.

The feathers will dry in the drain. If a window breaks in the late season storms, it will stay broken. When winter comes, there will be no one to turn on the heat, and the pipes will freeze. They will burst. She listens through the wall and the sounds of her parents slowly breathing softens into all the other living sounds of the summer evening. Into the crickets, into the hot wind, and into the solemn buzz of flies who will smile in the henhouse dirt. She will lock the door behind her. The chickens will become other things. She wipes her hands on a dish towel and then folds it, returns it to the countertop. Her hand rests on the towel. She can buy gas out of town, where no one knows her. She squares the edge of the dish towel with the counter and locks the door behind her. She stands still on the dark porch, licking the dust from each tooth. In years, the coop will fall in a storm and she will not fix it. She turns and unlocks the door again, and fills a glass and takes it into the bedroom. Her parents are in a place between sleep and life. She holds a turkey baster and pushes this into their mouths. She cannot ever seem to do this without knocking her mother's teeth. The sound is like a skull breaking on the ground. She feeds her parents water.

KATHERINE CART *is a candidate for an MFA in Creative Writing at the University of Virginia and holds a BS in General Biology from the University of New Hampshire. Before returning to academia to study literature, she worked in the commercial fisheries of the Bering Sea and Gulfs of Maine and Alaska. She is now quite interested in how the stories of extractive economies are getting told. Her writing is published or forthcoming in* The Masters Review *and* Raritan.

Stillborn

Isabelle Shifrin

It was a 110-degree day in early August, and I was bringing ice cream to the workers in the peppermint distillery when my uncle tore into the main building, Regina running behind him yelling over the equipment's cacophony about where was the first aid kit and why wasn't it where it was supposed to be. My uncle, briefly detained, it seemed, by the dimness inside the building, stumbled forward and into the light of the anemic bulb that hung from the ceiling. His face was collapsed below the eyeline into an Edvard Munch-like mask of white and puke green, his mouth a black sinkhole. My gaze fell down to the limp hand he held at chest height, and I registered in the distillery's gloom a smear of colors that reminded me of a desert sunset.

He grabbed an ice cream sandwich from me and held it against the back of his hand. Almost immediately melted ice cream began to seep through the corners of the paper package and run down his arm.

For a few seconds after the frozen treat touched his appendage, his features realigned themselves into some semblance of normalcy. But when he lifted the ice cream sandwich to see beneath it, all the skin from the back of his hand, pleated and sculpted as a yellowish tissue paper rose, slid to one side, revealing an angry, wet pink surface, mottled with patches of dry, dark red and oozing, orangish-white. He swallowed, shut his eyes and quickly replaced the treat on the wound.

Regina, apparently having exhausted all efforts to find the first aid kit, came up behind him. "What are you doing?" She shook her head in disbelief and smacked the ice cream sandwich away. She draped over the injured hand a bag of ice one of the workers had fetched from the farmhouse kitchen. "Les, you gotta go to clinic."

"Don't stop harvest," he gasped. "Niecie'll take me."

Luckily, the service pickup was parked nearby. Its driver's side door had been rammed in the previous winter by an anxious mother cow after my uncle took her baby inside the cab to warm it and administer electrolytes. I got into the passenger side. The hot vinyl seat pulled at the bare skin on the backs of my thighs as I skooched over behind the wheel. Regina and Hector helped my uncle in next to me.

We boiled down Three Mile Road among hundreds of acres of redolent green peppermint fields, many already cut but some not, as he took hissing breaths through gritted teeth. When we got to the highway I gunned it between hairpin turns that wended through the scorching basalt canyons near our farm, where on summer mornings hawks wheeled in the sky above the black rimrocks and scabby, barren white dirt hills. We emerged from the canyons into a landscape so large and empty it seemed to bleed through the truck windows and suck at our minds. My uncle's shoulders next to me, curved forward in pain, carried the same shape as the desert bluffs seen far in the distance through the windshield.

I didn't try to speak to him, just let him concentrate on managing his suffering.

Sometime later, it could have been one hour or a million, we fishtailed into the parking lot the clinic shared with the offices of the local peppermint commission in Douglas. The traveling nurse waited for us just inside the door. Regina had called in from the farmhouse phone to alert her we were on our way. She took the bag of tepid water that used to be ice from my uncle's wound and dropped it with precision into a trash can near the tiny reception desk.

Then she brought us down the hall to the examining room and bade me sit on the plastic lawn chair outside while she cleaned the wound. I bit at lips numbed with shock while I listened to sounds of a faucet running and my uncle's groans coming from behind the closed door. I heard the nurse say, "Steam hose spat boilin' water on your hand? Boiler must be broke then," and remembered hearing somewhere she was originally from only a few towns away, that she too came from a peppermint farming family.

After a little while my uncle emerged from the room, his hand bandaged so thickly it looked like the end of a Q-tip. His face was still haggard though, and his eyes clouded with suffering. The nurse followed him closely, her fingers pressed against her mouth in consternation. "That scalding water must've had some pressurized steam with it, I think, because it got you good. And it had all that time to fester on your way in with whatever that white slimy goo on it was." She frowned. He began to say something, and she waved him off. "I don't even want to know. We got most of it cleaned off anyway. Gave you the antibiotic." She held out a small bottle of pills. "I know you didn't want the shot in there. And you probably don't have time to drive up to Boise to fill a prescription, so I'm giving you some of the pain pills we have in stock."

My uncle, though, refused to take the pills. Incredulity spread across the nurse's face. "Those are second- and third-degree burns, Les."

He remained expressionless, but I saw the tiny spasm in the skin next to his eye. "We're in the thick of harvest, Cheryl. Surely you can understand."

Her mouth pursed, like she was going to say something more, but instead she nodded a little, as if coming to some private conclusion. Suddenly, she turned to me. She pressed the bottle into my hand and told me, "Just take them along, in case. Worse comes to worse, at least you'll have them."

As we left she called out, "Watch for fevers. And I want you back here in a day or so, to check for infection." Then, after a pause, "Like any farmer, your mind resides at least partly in your hands, Les. You got to take care of your hands."

I had a sudden mental image of her at the Koffee Kup Café in downtown Douglas, drinking watered-down Folgers and spouting folksy bits of wisdom like this one to a Farmers' Almanac kind of crowd. My uncle simply rolled his eyes.

On the way out of town, we drove by the One Stop, where a group of my schoolmates was congregated around the tailgate of a pickup truck, eating tater tots from paper boats and drinking from giant Styrofoam cups. Our farm was so far out on the desert I only interacted with people my age during the school year, and then only when I could manage to flex the flimsy, atrophied muscle of social interaction.

The people I knew were all perfectly nice to me, perfectly normal, but I couldn't focus on them. They could be talking to me, but I would be listening for the wind sweeping through the canyons. Sometimes, there was a nearly subaudible lilt of stars beyond the blue veil of sky, or a scent of basaltic sand mixed with rattlesnake piss.

My teachers wrote on my report cards that I was "remarkably inattentive."

"Yeah, but all the best farmers have ADD," Regina said when I told her.

It was kind of amazing, the things she would come up with to make me feel better.

What was in those Styrofoam cups my peers drank from, I wondered now, glancing at them as we passed. Milkshakes, probably. Ice cream. The thought made my stomach roil. At the same time, a sudden desire for whatever it was they might be drinking overcame me. That was living, I thought. Whatever it was they were doing, laughing, having fun with each other. That was real life, like the kind I sometimes glimpsed in ads in the months-old magazines they stocked in the Douglas grocery store.

"She has a nice butt," my uncle observed. His voice dull with pain.

At his words, my stomach went from roil to lurch, and bile shot into my throat. Daniela Manzanares, who was in my grade, stood with her back to the street as we passed.

We drove the rest of the way to the farm without speaking. From time to time, I glanced sideways at Uncle Les, trying to gauge his mood. I saw no telling signal in his expression, nothing like the eye twitch I had seen in the clinic. Yet the shadowed line of his profile seemed somehow sharper than usual against the blonde, cheatgrass-covered desert that rolled out beyond him through the truck window like a great dirt sea.

His words about Daniela persisted in the cab's stuffy, silent air. It occurred to me I'd heard something extra in them, some mixture of rage and disgust. Had I also sensed something like accusation? Was he simply off-kilter from his injury, or was there something more complicated happening? I wondered if I had done something wrong, without being aware.

When we arrived back at the distillery, he instructed me to park next to the discharge ditch. He grabbed from the truck dashboard the bottle of pain pills. Then he got out of the truck, opened the bottle and poured its contents into the warmish water that ran back into the river. He tossed the empty bottle into the truck bed and went into the farmhouse without a glance in my direction.

I got out of the truck and collapsed on the lawn to wait for him. When he emerged again a few moments later, he held a cold Dr. Pepper in his good hand. I knew it was for me, a random can he must've found in the back of the fridge where I'd missed it after blowing through this week's six-pack. He wouldn't want it for himself. He thought Dr. Pepper tasted like cough syrup.

I reached up for the soda. Instead of handing it down to me though, he stared intently at the horizon for a second, in a way that made me think he was weighing options. "'Turning and turning in the widening gyre,'" he intoned. "'Things fall apart; the centre cannot hold.'" His nostrils flared as he murmured, "Yep, it's all lost to entropy in the end."

The way he spoke, as though he were an actor in some play, as though he assumed I were looking up at him from the audience, enthralled, suddenly irritated me on a gut level. Also, I was dreading he'd fuck up the lines. The evening before, he'd bade me, as I was leaving the farmhouse to check for clogs in the irrigation lines, "'Go gently into that good night, do not rage against the dying of your might.'"

When I had tried to correct him, he'd only raised an eyebrow, and it had come over me that he was deconstructing the poem, in a way that somehow defiled it, or negated it, or reverted it to figment, on purpose, simply because he could. This had irked me so much I'd had a brief fantasy of coldcocking him in the side of the head. The violence of the image, my fist connecting with the hard side of his face, had first startled me and then made me feel incredibly guilty.

Finally, as though reaching some cul-de-sac in his mental roving, Uncle Les handed the soda down to me. I took it with relief and popped open the tab.

He said, "I think I got some of them extra-thick leather, elbow-length safety gloves out in the shop we can use for changing out the steam hoses from here on out."

"So we're not going to fix whatever's wrong?"

"Nope. We only got a week of harvest left. We're gonna limp on through."

I thought about reminding him of his own maxim: "When something's broke, you shut it down until it can be mended." But I said nothing. Time was of the essence during harvest, even I knew that.

"I ain't gonna be able to work clear through to closing today with this injury though," he said. "Pain's suckin' me dry."

"You need me to cover you at the still for your usual shift after Regina leaves, six pm 'til midnight," I supplied. Probably I should have been a little pissed off that he, a grown man and supposedly my protector, would dump such a dangerous burden into my lap. Like many 16-year-old farm kids living in southern Idaho at that time, the time before internet and cell phones and even CDs, I could operate almost anything, swathers and balers and all manner of tractors. But I had never once worked a whole shift as distillery operator by myself, and, though I knew how, I'd never once put the still to bed by myself either.

My first inclination however, was relief. Even if he wouldn't shut down the still, even if he wouldn't take the pain pills, he at least knew he needed to rest a few hours. And who else could he turn to? Besides Regina, who had to leave right at six so she could get home to care for her livestock, no one else was trained on distillery operation but me.

But as I took a first sip of the Dr. Pepper, the sensation of cold liquid moving down my throat and spreading across my chest brought not pleasure, but a sense of impending doom.

Uncle Les seemed to sense my unease. Affection and sorriness mingled with the suffering in the depths of his brown eyes. "Tell you what I'll do. I'll change up the system just for tonight, have the mint tub drivers hook and unhook the steam hoses for yuh. So you won't have to mess with any of the steam lines. Just stay inside the main building and run the gauges."

I nodded. It was helpful that the grownups would change out the hoses. It took away some of the danger.

But not all.

I licked the corners of my mouth, tasting faint traces of the Dr. Pepper's sweetness in the dried crust there. "Would it be possible to wake up and come help me shut down the boiler at midnight?"

The nurse's words to my uncle in the examining room had stayed in the back of my mind throughout the drive home. When you thought about it, it wasn't the hoses, uncomplicated appendages, that were the cause of the earlier calamity. You had to trace the steam, or scalding water, as the case may be, back to its source. Back to the boiler.

My uncle, seeming to intuit my fear, made a short, exasperated sound. "It's not gonna blow!"

But then he grinned wolfishly.

"What's wrong with it, do you think?" I pressed.

He shrugged, and now I glimpsed a new surge of his irritability. "Gotta be the skimmer pipe's broke." He shook his head in disgust, as if he couldn't believe life had dealt him this card.

The afternoon was already waning as he took off on the four-wheeler, awkwardly depressing the throttle with the forearm above his bandage, to check the fields one last time before retreating to the farmhouse to rest. I finished up my Dr. Pepper and headed across the driveway.

Regina sat on the ratty couch just inside the still door, reading the latest copy of the D&B Supply catalog.

Maybe sensing my presence in the doorway, Regina glanced up and smiled. "You puttin' the still to bed tonight?"

I nodded and sat down on the couch arm. Then I asked, half shouting to be heard over the still's din, "Did you have to hook up any more hoses while we were gone to the clinic?"

"We had to do one tub. I wrapped my regular work gloves in shop towels and Braulio found an old piece of cardboard in the shop and held it up like a shield while we brought the hose up and undid the camlock. But nothin' happened.

"Yer uncle stopped by here on his way to check the field, told me he thinks the way the boiler's broke, them hoses might only shoot steam and scaldin' water every now and again. Not in a way we can predict."

She got up and went over to the fifty-gallon barrel closest to us to check the level of mint oil inside. When she came back to the couch, wiping oily fingers on the legs of her Wranglers, I saw the concentration of menthol had made her weep. "This batch is strong stuff! Them toothpaste companies are gonna love it!"

She flopped back down on the cushions. "He told me he ain't takin' that pain medication either. Can't say as I blame him for not takin' the prescription pain pills, all that's goin' on. He'll need to stay sharp. Still, he could at least take an ibuprofen or a Tylenol maybe. His hand must hurt like hell."

"You know he doesn't like pills," I replied.

Regina nodded, and we fell to silence. But before she left, she told me, "I made a promise to myself when yer mama went that I'd always look out for you." She grew thoughtful and chewed on her lip. "You was just a little red-faced thing when you was born, looked just like a skinned jackrabbit. And no one knew who yer daddy was. And yer mama just a teenager." She clucked her tongue and then leveled her gaze at me. "I'd put on some jeans if I was you."

"Les said the drivers would use safety gloves to change out the steam for me while I run the gauges inside the building."

She nodded again, but still I thought she looked faintly troubled.

When she left, I watched the dust cloud behind her truck grow smaller and smaller as it traveled the desolate length of road, before finally disappearing at the highway. Her small farm was seven miles from ours, and was arrived at by traveling through a series of crumbling basalt canyons. Something about her manner as she departed, a grimness at odds with her personality, left me even more unsettled than I had been before.

I turned back to the still after she'd gone. Before I could stop myself, I glanced sideways to see a sliver of the boiler's flank visible between two ten-foot-tall condensers. It was only a small expanse of dull, unimposing steel, yet I held within my mind a vision of the boiler in all its terrible totality. Seen from its front or from the opposite side of the distillery, where the view of it was not obstructed by a row of condensers, the boiler's true dimensions and character emerged. It was nearly twice my height and twenty-five feet long, an enormous steel, potbellied boar whose front end sprouted strange, circuitous metal tubing like fat face piercings.

As though the boiler were thinking about me too, it layered a new growl over its ever-present, baseline lament. The ceiling bulb flickered. I knew it was only a matter of electricity, the voltage flowing to the bulb diminishing a little as the boiler drew more. Probably it was only clocking the presence of the tub Regina and Braulio had most recently attached to it. Still, foreboding puddled between my shoulders like ice water.

I didn't think my uncle would knowingly put me in harm's way, even if he was out of his mind with suffering and sleep deprivation. His encyclopedic knowledge of the distillery remained intact. He had named the problem. It was the skimmer pipe, the skinny tube that pulled all the extra calcium and undissolved solids from the water in the boiler's gut so it could flash to steam.

Like he said, a broken skimmer pipe could not cause a boiler to blow. It could not crack the steel shell, making the internal pressure briefly rocket to 2,500,000 pounds per square inch as it went atmospheric, causing the machine's innards to melt like chocolate, steam-cooking anyone within a hundred feet.

Yet, after a moment, the sense of relief deserted me. I had noticed something strange happening with my thoughts recently. Sometimes, reality and rational things no longer had any authority inside my mind. And now, try as I might, I could not make my brain believe I was safe.

In part to calm myself, I got a handful of Doritos from the open bag on the distillery cupboard's filthy countertop. I knew the Doritos would taste like mentholated corn chips, any remnant of nacho cheese having long since been erased by the environs. But I was determined to finish them. After all, eating junk food was what normal teenagers did. I cradled the handful against my midsection and sat back down, reaching for the book Regina had loaned me to pass the time while the mint cooked throughout the evening. It was a romance paperback whose cover showed a tall man with a sardonic grin and cruel eyes sheltering a young woman inside his cape during a lightning storm.

I found I couldn't concentrate on the novel though, not even when the heroine grew gravely ill and the hero with the asshole personality finally realized how much he truly loved her.

Then, after only an hour and a half had passed since I'd begun my shift and it was still light outside, my uncle came through the doorway. I realized I wasn't completely surprised to see him, with his drawn, gray face, his curly hair disheveled. Even considering his terrible shape, the idea of him resting longer than a few hours during harvest time had always seemed improbable. The pressure was too intense. An entire year's worth of planning and plotting came to fruition, or didn't, during a handful of weeks. There were hundreds of thousands of dollars in play.

I watched him make the rounds inside the distillery. He rechecked gauges whose positions I had already noted, and perused the clipboard that recorded the number of inches of mint oil each tub produced. After a moment, he sat down heavily next to me on the couch, holding his bandaged hand gingerly against his chest.

"Wachu readin?" With his good hand he reached across me, to grab my novel from where it sat on the couch arm. He had begun to insist that summer on reading everything I read, including those poetry and art books Regina had bought for me at the library sale in Boise back in June.

A glimmer of interest lit his pain-dulled eyes while he looked over the romance novel.

"Only a silly book," I replied.

Abruptly, he put the novel back on the couch arm. Then he reached over again. I looked down to see he had placed his well hand on the pale, bare flesh of my very upper thigh, just below the hem of my shorts.

Time and repetition of that gesture and others of varying trespass would reveal different shades of meaning in that initial moment. But really, the moment itself was the largest nesting doll without the rest of the set, totally empty. At that point, it contained nothing but itself. His hand on my thigh even felt pleasant. It was as though he were claiming me, and there was comfort in that. I inhaled traces of the beloved scent emanating from his flank, the familiar, almost-metallic tone of his sweat.

I remembered a photo we had, that he kept in a shoebox with other family photos, in the storage closet under the farmhouse stairs. In it, he crouched in front of the farmhouse, holding a baby me on his knee, my infant's back resting in the crook of his arm. Both of us were dressed to the nines, and he held a folder in one hand he later told me contained his copy of the kinship adoption papers. I looked wobbly but content in that photo. And fat! I had been such a deliciously, joyfully fat baby. My uncle attributed my hyperbolic growth to the fact he had not given me baby formula after the sudden postpartum death of his sister, my mother, from eclampsia. Ever the iconoclast, he had instead paid a breastfeeding mother in Douglas to provide breastmilk for me in sterilized glass bottles. So bizarre and unbelievable was this arrangement, in that time and place, that as my extra chins bloomed and the rolls of my thighs multiplied, the elderly women in Douglas gossiped that my uncle was actually feeding me cream from his heifers.

"Women are real bitches sometimes," he'd told me later, the first time he relayed the story of my baby chub. "All they really want, is to manipulate the situation. Like, sometimes they let their tits hang halfway out their tube tops and then make a fuss when someone tries to cop a feel."

I, who was about five at the time, laughed along with him, sensing no danger to myself.

Anyway, the women of Douglas were soon quieted. My baby fat melted into the lean legs of childhood as I trotted and ran barefoot along ditch banks to keep up with my uncle, a cloth doll he had fashioned for me from some old Butterick sewing pattern tucked under my arm.

In the still, sitting next to him on the couch, I daydreamed of running into the woman in town who had given up her milk for the infant me. "I drank your breastmilk," I might say, "but now everything tastes like peppermint."

"Fun fact," I might tell her. "Commercial grade peppermint oil is not delicious. Just a small amount will burn your tongue, blow out your sinuses, make your mouth numb."

I bit my lips, thinking of numbness.

The wall of sound pulsing from the boiler seemed to separate, petulance and rage and loneliness and sorrow becoming distinct. My thoughts rested on the Morris tube inside the boiler. This canal, as long as the boiler and big enough around to hold a person, housed the first pass of fire, a tremendous, 2,000-degree flame that was almost as powerful as a jet afterburner. It was what gave the boiler its formidable sound.

How might it feel to be somehow trapped inside that intractable steel tube? It was a strange thought, shooting like a bolt of white across my mind. A sensation of intense, paralyzing claustrophobia bled over me. I struggled inwardly, but couldn't seem to move, to escape from the couch, from under my uncle's hand.

"Yep, it's supposed to be above 110 degrees for the next few days yet," he said suddenly. "I don't even care. Mint likes it." He snorted in derision, as if even something as beyond our control and complex as weather had nothing on him.

To my surprise, his words began to press and press at me, in a way that made me feel precariously cleaved into some kind of thin strata. Each translucent layer of myself, fragile as hardened dermis, began to shift and slide back and forth, as though displaced by the boiler's immense roar, until I caught a glimpse of a plate near the bottom of them all, numinous and ancient, radiating phosphorescent blackened indigo.

To be wounded at such a root level, by such a casual comment about the weather, confused and then galled me. I gazed at that well hand, sweating against my thigh, and tried to connect it with some understanding. Under the powerful smell of menthol, the weak though abiding smell of overcooked cellulose, a cloying, putrid scent of boiling plant after all the mint oil has been distilled from it, filled the back of my throat.

When my voice finally emerged, my words surprised me. "Why did you throw away them pain pills Cheryl gave you?"

If Les was taken aback by this question, he didn't show it. "Can't manage harvest if yer loopy. And don't start about ibuprofen. Don't need it and it's bad for my kidneys."

Now my voice shot out, urgent and even enraged. "Maybe you should at least take some of them other pills you're supposed to be taking when there's a lot of stress, from that special doc up in Boise."

His features went rigid except for the corner of his mouth, which began subtly to lift into a snarl, as though the very mention of the meds filled him with disgust. "You and Regina. I'll make the changes I need to without pills."

He tilted his head to look again at the romance novel where it rested on the couch arm. "I heard if yuh masturbate it makes hair grow on yer palms."

Without thinking, I held up my hands and looked at my palms. He began to chuckle and my face grew hot. I moved away from him and his hand slid to the couch between us.

I stood and said, "I'm going to make coffee. Do you want any?"

He nodded a little and grimaced, as if suddenly recalled to his suffering by my inquiry.

Outside the distillery, I forgot for a moment where I was going. My tired eyes followed the scribbled line of desert plain and bluff, where there called out to me some mystery, constantly renewing itself. Was Daniela Manzanares out there on the desert somewhere? I wondered. Still with her companions, but now, having finished their milkshakes, bundled under the stars, drinking Rumple Minze?

Away from the boiler's noise, the landscape seemed absolutely still and silent, but also expectant. Poised somehow. Liminal. I raised one callused hand and traced the long blade of the horizon, waiting for the idea I knew would arrive: He was probably not a monster. He was not navigable by anyone but himself, but he was not a monster. There was love beneath that he could not access at the moment. In spite of everything, I thought I could feel that love, faintly pulsing like a vein below the skin, the muscle, the fascia.

My eye fell from the horizon to the discharge ditch nearby. I began to search the weeds along the bank until I found two or three errant pain pills of the bunch the nurse had given. These I brought into the farmhouse.

While a pot of coffee was brewing in the farmhouse kitchen, I rummaged in my uncle's medicine cabinet until I found the pill bottles I needed. Following the directions on the bottle labels, I crushed into a little bowl with the back of a spoon three of one kind of pill and three of another the doc up in Boise had prescribed for him. I added two crushed pain pills to this mixture and poured it into his cup of coffee, stirring until I felt sure it had all dissolved.

I brought the coffee back out to the distillery. When something was broke, I considered, you shut it down until it was fixed. I could not finish harvest alone, but Regina and I could run the mint distillery a day or two, safety precautions in place, while my uncle slept and his hand began to heal.

He took a sip of the hot liquid and said, "Jeez. So bitter. 'Bout took my tongue off."

"I brewed it strong," I replied.

He took another sip and his gaze turned contemplative. "I know you think I'm stupid."

I sat back down at the opposite end of the couch and looked at him. "I don't think you're stupid. I just think you're an ass sometimes."

His face went pale with fury.

"You don't know how good you got it," he hissed. "My dad beat the shit out of me every day of my life until I was fourteen. At least I show you affection."

"You're not my father," I said.

"Am I not? No one knows, do they?"

I considered that maybe I should've added more medicine to the coffee mixture.

In spite of his fury, he was beginning to be sleepy. I watched his face relax by degrees, watched his chin dip a little towards his chest. He looked at me with deep sorrow and said, "You know, yuh got me, Niecie. Even if no one else will ever love you or understand you. Even if you go to a city and no one knows your name. If they think yer weird or a yokel. If they can tell yer broken but they don't how. Yuh got me."

I caught him as he fell sideways and, straining with effort, laid him on the couch without disturbing his bandaged hand. I picked up his feet and legs and moved them to the couch as well, so he was lying comfortably.

I got myself an empty five-gallon bucket from the shop and flipped it over for a seat. The hours passed, the peppermint cooked. He slept, auburn curls plastered to the side of his face with sweat. At midnight, I went to the back of the still and turned a knob on the boiler's face to "idle." It did not grow more quiet, but deep within the machine's bowels a note changed, went from sorrow to resolution. My fear for the boiler seemed to now exist on a different plane, not accessible from where I was. It was almost like I suddenly didn't care, how dangerous it was or if it would kill me or whatever. With a calm that was almost boredom, I followed the rest of the boiler shutdown steps.

The last thing to do was flip a switch that finally extinguished the flame inside the machine. With a great whoosh, the beast went still. In the ensuing silence, more profound than actual silence, I thought maybe it was normal. The way he'd put his hand on my thigh. There were worse things to survive. I recalled a numbness during that interval of trespass that was, not nice exactly, but safe. Or safe-ish. I recalled a certain diffusion of my senses. And within the diffusion, the cold scent of sagebrush, the basalt cliffs like shards scraping the sky, a sense of relinquishment, or maybe a sigh, moving across the top of the nearby peppermint fields as they began to wilt, telling me they'd need to be cut soon, or watered, or fed.

ISABELLE SHIFRIN *is a Boise-based writer of flash fiction, short fiction and nonfiction. A graduate of Columbia University's Graduate School of Journalism and an attendee of the Iowa Writers' Workshop summer session, her nonfiction has appeared in* The Idaho Statesman *and* Newsday. *Her short fiction has been featured in* The Missouri Review, *and her most recent flash fiction was shortlisted for the* Fractured Lit 2022 Winter Fast Flash Challenge. *She is currently working on a novel that explores the intersection of water rights, eating disorders and aliens. You can read more of Isabelle's work at Isabelleshifrin.com.*

Spider Tim

Leah Edwards

When Florida's ChimpanZOO rescued a litter of spider monkeys from a breeder's illegal operation in Waco, Texas, only one survived: Tim. Max held the baby monkey and said, "Just Tim is not cool. Let's call him Spider Tim."

I watched Max bottle feed Spider Tim, dabbing dribbled Similac from his soft brown fur. Spider Tim slept against Max's chest, in an Ergobaby carrier, while Max worked, Scotch taping the jaws of gator hatchlings, hacking up raw poultry. Tucking his sweat-drenched, shoulder-length brown hair behind his ear, lobe stretched two inches wide. Wiping his face with the half sleeve of his green, PROTECT THE MANATEES shirt. Sometimes (a lot of times) the orangutan, Sally, flung fresh feces at the back of Max's head. Max turned, always said, "Hey, come on now, Sal." I fell in love with him again and again and again.

He taught the primates American Sign Language. He signed, *Are you happy here?*

No.

He turned to me. Signed, *Lola, Are you happy here?*

"No."

"What would make you happy?"

"I don't know."

I wasn't at ChimpanZOO by choice, not at first—I was a court-mandated ChimpanTEER. Public intoxication. Public urination. You've never peed on the TECO streetcar after getting Jager'ed at Ybor—good for you. The social worker told me: "If you learn how to take care of others, you can learn how to take care of yourself."

I said, "So the oxygen mask goes on the monkey first?"

"That's right, Lola. Exactly."

If I had known ASL then, I would have signed, *bullshit, Kathy*. I would have signed that at AA, too, when they sang their slogans. I taught those slogans to the caged, wing-clipped parrots:

Progress, not perfection. That's right!

Let go and let God. That's it!

For the primates, I fermented their fruit. Those peaches, pomegranates, and apricots were second only to the kids' toys Max pulled from curbside trash piles: Furbies, Cabbage Patch Kids, a Bop It. The Bop It, they considered that a gift from God, from Max. Max tried to be a good God, spending his entire paycheck, one month, on liquidated stock from Toys "R" Us. But all the monkeys wanted were Bop Its. To cradle the hard plastic rod against their chest, to press the speaker to their ear, for the beloved *boing*.

So the day that Spider Tim impaled Max in the left eye with a battery-dead Bop It, we were all shocked. I was with the gators, dangling a hunk of skinned rabbit off of a fishing rod, when I heard Max scream. But wait, I'll start at the beginning.

* * *

The first time I heard Max scream was in the Tampa ER, when the nurse stuck a tube down his throat to begin pumping his stomach. I pulled back the curtain that separated us, watched the contents of his liquored gut empty into a hazardous waste bag. When he could talk, he turned to me and said, "That was fucking gross."

"No kidding."

He asked me what I was there for. "Mifepristone."

Hours passed. The nurse came back into the room, pushed the curtain closed. "Lola, that's not the type of thing we can prescribe. You need to go to Planned Parenthood. Tallahassee."

"Tallahassee? Then D and C me. This is kind of a, you know, emergency."

"That's not how it works. Not here. This isn't an emergency."

It was 11:54 PM. At 2:02 PM, I was at my boyfriend's apartment. He, Skip, was pressing my cheek to the stove's gas cooktop, to a burner crusted with yesterday's scrambled eggs. He fingered the stove knob, threatening to brand me, to light my yellow hair on fire.

We stood like that until 2:34 PM—"I'll punch ya in the gut, Lola, kick ya so hard the baby'll fall right outta you." I looked around his shithole apartment and counted things—the vintage, black and white Weeki Wachee posters. Amber beer bottles full of the plastic wrap from cigarette boxes. Mickey Mouse figurines that he collected from Happy Meals, then disfigured on the barbecue, flattening them into pucks of black, white, and red, one dash of yellow. One crocheted blanket of the American flag. Two handguns. Three semi-feral cats.

He let me go. Smoked up then passed out on the couch watching Dr. Drew. And I turned to the kitchen sink, threw up everything—everything inside of me except what I couldn't—and left. Took the TECO streetcar to the ER.

"Yeah," I said to the nurse. "It is, this is an emergency for me."

"I can get you something to help you relax."

"I don't need—"

"Look, Lola—"

"Can't you just prescribe—"

"Think about it, Lol."

She said my name, abbreviated, like she was laughing at me. Want a medical abortion? Lol. Good fucking luck getting to Tallahassee, honey—no streetcar runs that far. And an Uber? LOL, that'll cost you at least two fifty.

When the nurse dipped, Max split the curtain. He said, "Grab that benzos script for me and I'll drive ya up to Tally."

* * *

He pulled up in a blue Sebring. The back windows were busted, covered in cardboard and duct tape. The nurse who wouldn't prescribe me mifepristone was outside, on a break. Dragging on a cigarette, chugging down a Monster. Looked at me like, *Girl, don't get in that car.* But I wasn't afraid of Max's janky Sebring. I was afraid of my own body—what it was, what it could have become, if I didn't get in the car right then.

Max said, "Ready for a road trip, ER roomie?"

"Lola."

"Lola, cool."

"Can we swing through a Taco Bell drive through?"

"You magic Mickey mind reader—swear to God I was just thinking of how good a Black Bean Chalupa Supreme would taste right now."

We got a double of the Chalupa Supreme, sat on the Sebring's hood and dripped taco sauce onto the asphalt. Got back into the car where Max said, "Hey Siri, map me to Planned Parenthood."

Okay, I'm mapping you to Palm Harbor.

"No, bitch. *Planned Pa-rent-hood.*"

Okay, I'm mapping you to Planned Parenthood.

"That's right."

And we were off, off to Tallahassee.

* * *

Driving up the I-75, at ninety miles an hour, Max said, "This is kinda the opposite of what I use'ta do."

"What was that?"

"Artificially inseminating dairy cows."

"Jesus."

"Yep, spent all day thawing semen, my arm gloved up and inside a cow. Until they canned me for fucking up one insemination pretty bad." He took a swig of Pepsi. "It really messed me up. I went full PETA vegan."

"So what do you do now? For, like, work."

"Man, not much."

"McDonalds isn't hiring?"

"Even McDonalds won't let felons make Happy Meals. But I'm looking for work. I'm looking."

Max turned on the radio, except it wasn't the radio, it was a CD he'd burned. It skipped, skipped, played. Ben Bridwell's horses clip-clopped into the Sebring. Max sang along to the first few lines, chewing on a lime-flavored TUMS. It was his fifth, his sixth.

I said to Max, "I know a place that's hiring. They'll take anyone, almost—alcoholics, felons."

"Oh yeah?"

"Yeah." He passed me an orange TUMS. "How do you feel about primates?"

* * *

We played truth or dare, but because we were two strangers, blasting down the interstate, both with fucked up bodies, we were already in a dare. So it was all truth. Max went first.

Truth: His childhood nickname was Tropicana, because his parents beat him to a pulp. He was charged with second degree arson in 2003, for burning down their house, a Sarasota bungalow.

Truth: I haven't just peed on streetcars, in public. I've fallen down stairs, thrown punches. Been on the other side of the curtain one, two, three—skip to nine—times, getting my gut pumped. It is genetic, someone told me: come from drunks, end up a drunk. There's no hope for you, Lol. It's what you are.

Truth: That when Max lit the fire, he didn't realize it was just Slurpee, his blind dog, still in the house. "I got two years, then 300 hours of community service. I've cleaned a lot of busted tires and roadkill from this highway." He told me about the opossum organs melted onto Florida asphalt. Smears of bladders, spleens. "And I'm definitely, most certainly, one hundred percent going direct to hell for killing that sweet, visionless beagle."

Truth: I would never be a mother, even if I wanted to be, because that is nine months—a purple chip, an impossible thing. Kathy had asked me, "Do you have a support system?"

What do you think, Kath? My parents live in Tampa, nine miles down the road. I never see them. They are Gasparilla pirates, wearing eye patches and *arrrr*'ing with fake parrots on their shoulders one week out of the year. The other fifty-one weeks they collect fraudulent disability checks. Run scams. Beg on the Tampa strip. They were born here, I was born here, but we don't exist in the same Sunshine State. They are gone. Gone since they kicked me out at sixteen with a "Hey, good luck" and forty bucks and "Just get a boyfriend, anyone, who'll take care of you." Dappled, now, in Skip-scars that the sun makes darker.

It is what I am.

* * *

It took two appointments, twenty-four hours apart. So Max and I stayed at Motel 6 on Apalachee Parkway, just down the street from The Moon.

Max split a benzo with a 7-Eleven rewards card. "You want half?"

"Yeah."

We lay in separate beds, watched episodes of *Friday Night Lights*, imagining that the American South was a place other than what it is—busted guts scattered on interstates. Women's bodies that belong to men. Animal bodies impregnated again and again and again.

Max fell asleep first, and I opened a Bible. Thumbed through it. Then I opened a Florida Travel and Tourism Guidebook: *Explore the Sunshine State!* I placed the black and white ultrasound photo, the contents of my womb, between Walt Disney World and Weeki Wachee Springs State Park. Mice and mermaids. Said: I'm sorry? Godspeed? I didn't know—good enough.

* * *

Max held my hand.

"Is this your partner? Your spouse?"

"No."

"I'm her ER roomie."

"He drove me here."

"So he's your support person."

"Sure."

I closed my eyes and counted the primates at ChimpanZOO: one spider monkey, two spider monkeys, three spider monkeys, four. Five to 600—it was done. I don't like to talk about it.

On the drive home, I told Max about ChimpanZOO. "The orangutang wants to be a musician. The spider monkeys watched *Jackass* and now they ghost ride their Little Tikes bikes into the pond of septic water. We have to give them bleach baths. It pays seventeen an hour. And Max, Max."

"Yeah, Lola?"

I was so dosed out on lorazepam, kept repeating, "The monkeys will love you. Max, the monkeys will love you. They'll love you."

"Oh yeah?"

"Yeah. They'll fall in love with you."

We passed blue and orange Gainesville. Passed the Crystal River. Eighty miles an hour. South towards Tampa, towards Tarpon Springs. Cardboard windows flapping. We were starved, but hadn't passed a fast-food joint in miles. Wouldn't for miles more. Didn't have any money left, anyway. I needed something to fill me, so I said, "Tell me, again, about how you burned your parents' house down. But this time, Max, start at the beginning, with where you bought the lighter fluid."

* * *

"Lola!"

I was dangling a hunk of skinned rabbit off of a fishing rod and into the gator pond when I heard Max scream. Making wishes. Wishing I could forgive my parents. Wishing that I didn't always cry when Max held my face in his hands and said, "I love this primate, you, Lola, most of all."

"Lola!"

Max was blood drenched. Debbie, senior amphibians' wrangler, started wrapping his head in paper towels, "Put these bad boys to the test, the greater picker upper, yeah, we'll see," as Cora, junior amphibians' wrangler, called 911, "That's right. I told you! I'm not making it up! We need an ambulance, like, now," and someone else, a guest I think, said to me, "Shouldn't you be making sure that the kids don't see this?" But I couldn't move, couldn't talk.

"Lola!"

Paramedics arrived, made their Florida Man jokes while administering fentanyl, dressing Max's head in sheets of gauze.

"Lola!"

Spider Tim dropped the Bop It. Reached, gently, towards Max.

Max was on a stretcher, blood still oozing from his eye socket and through the gauze, when he said, to a guest, "Jesus, fuck. Can you please stop feeding Simon cream cheese bagels. He's vegan."

Simon signed: *vegan.*

* * *

After Max's surgery, the owner of ChimpanZOO called, said, "You know, Max. You know I got to."

"That's a fucking lie," said Max, touching his bandaged eye. "Release him into the wild, release him to me."

"I can't."

"You can do whatever you want."

"That's not true."

Max held Spider Tim's hand as he was euthanized. Petted his soft fur and said, "It's not your fault. I'm sorry, Spider Tim, I'm sorry." I was signing *sorry* on loop, crying into a curly-haired Cabbage Patch Kid.

They buried him out back, in a little plot next to the dumpsters, with his favorite Fisher Price Little People figurine—a brown haired man with a green shirt.

ChimpanZOO got renamed—it's now the Florida Primate Rescue, and they were given 501(c)3 status. We don't work there anymore, but we go back to visit, and we have one of their bumper stickers: *We saw Singing Sally at the FPR!* Singing Sally plucks folk chords—Max taught her "Sink, Florida, Sink"—on an acoustic guitar. With her free hand, she pushes her fingers through the first chain link fence.

They started double caging the primates. That's right.

There are no more Bop Its. That's it.

At home, Max opens his Publix paycheck, then his medical bills. It cost a quarter of a million dollars for an ophthalmologist in Tampa to stick a glass orb in his left socket. Max pets my face and I can see myself—sixty days sober—reflected in his orb. He says that he sees it: one hundred days, then 200, then 300. "One day you *will* be happy, Lola. One day you will be happy." He places both hands in front of his chest, makes the sign for *happy*.

I can't be happy, not yet. I think constantly about the dead batteries, the fermented peaches. Tallahassee.

Let go? I don't think I can. Let God? Yeah right. But Max, he says, "Spin it, pull it, shout it—America sucks ass." Signs the check. Writes: *It's okay, Spider Tim* in the memo section and draws a tiny heart.

LEAH EDWARDS *is a graduate of the University of Toronto's Master's in English in the Field of Creative Writing program. Her short fiction has been published in* Room *and* Hazlitt. *She lived, briefly, in Dunedin, Florida, and now lives in Hamilton, Ontario. She is currently working on her first novel.*

The Swans

Daniel Monzingo

We came from across the world, the students of the No. 4 Affiliated International School, and we yearned—as all young do—for wild skies. I'd been at the school since sixth grade when my ABC parents returned to their Shanghai roots and brought me along, packed up with the clothes, the furniture, and dreams of new wealth in the old world. It was the last year of middle school, ninth grade. The year I met Omi.

He joined the school on Halloween, and the first time I saw him was in Mr. Joyce's literature class. He had on a stovepipe hat for his costume, his face painted like a *calavera*, and he was shooting the bird behind the teacher's back, all of it before anyone even knew his name. The brassier boys elbowed each other, chattering like parrots, and a couple of the girls twittered behind their hands. The rest of us gawped. When the teacher turned around to see what was happening, the skull-faced boy was sitting there with his painted-on smile, hands folded in his lap like a mummified monk, eyes shut serenely, betrayed only by one tiny snort. It was, I am sure, my first taste of love.

It was also just the beginning of the trouble he caused, and over the next month we got used to seeing his mom on campus, an elegant Mexican woman in a Chanel suit who worked at some nearby tech company. His dad was rumored to be Japanese, but no one ever saw him, the dad, not even the day Omi was expelled.

The ninth graders flocked around him like pigeons to crumbs, eating up his antics. They loved his vulgar proclamations, delivered in careless Mandarin, and sought reflections of themselves in his lunar light, neither Western nor Eastern but Other. All of them, that is, except me, for I did not dare approach.

One day I was in the office on an errand for the homeroom teacher when I heard Mr. Joyce say to Mrs. Adler, the writing teacher, "You can't help but like him a little, even if he is a pain in the ass." I knew they were talking about Omi, and I sipped like a hummingbird from the sugar water of their speech.

"No way. Kid's a prick. It's never good when they show up mid-semester."

"A rooster in a henhouse," said Dr. Wu over the cubicle wall.

"More like a snake," said Mrs. Adler.

Their conversation flapped off elsewhere, and I stopped listening. If seeing Omi had been my first taste of love, hearing him disparaged was my first taste of hate. What did any of them know about him? What did they know about any of us? I left the office, dragging my indignation behind me like a broken wing.

A fitful sleeper, I always rose with the lark, and my industrious parents dropped me off early on their way to the office. Omi, on the other hand, lived on campus, and I guessed his parents, like so many others, didn't want him around the house. Sometimes I arrived as he emerged from the dormitory, and I would watch him saunter towards the gym while I went to the classroom to read. I never could, when I knew he was there, and instead I daydreamed about what he did every morning in that rank and terrifying place.

A month later, at the end of November when the sweltering Shanghai heat finally fled and the last leaves turned to falling fire, I screwed up my courage and followed him into the gym. He must have known I was there, but he walked like he was the only thing in creation, cocksure and strapping, king of a kingdom he disdained, an exiled god serving sentence among the clay.

I got out my kit and half watched him changing from the corner of my eye. After the longest two minutes of my life, I slipped after him into the dusky realm of weight machines and braver boys. Omi was already on the bench press heaving a barbell up and down, moon-pale biceps flexing, the deep hollows beneath his shoulders slick with sweat. I bid my wary eye wander from those woods down to where another forest grew across the naked plains between his jersey and his sweatpants, but I lost my nerve, looked away, and focused on the kettle bell I was straining to lift before I let it fall with a frustrated clang.

Omi kept lifting like he hadn't heard a thing. I wandered among the machines, mysterious things meant for older boys, for men, and I tried to distract myself figuring out their functions, rattling them softly now and again like stacks of bones. The whole time, I kept glancing at Omi. The fluorescent lights sparkled on the sweat pearling his arms, his upper lip, the tips of his cartoon hair. I compared the lushness of his armpits to the fauny down dusting mine, and my yen rode the rolling swell of his chest like a seabird in a storm.

Metal rang on metal and Omi sat up, panting. His eyes transfixed me where I stood ruminating and fiddling with the hot handlebar of a BowFlex, "You wanna try it?" he asked.

I'd have given anything just then to crawl out of my skin and ooze onto the floor with the rest of the slime. Instead, I looked away and shook my head. Omi shrugged and tossed sweat from his hair. Then he considered me again from the end of the bench where he sat with his satyr's legs splayed, green gaze moving over me like a butcher guessing weight. Just before I lost my nerve again, he said, "You wanna see something?"

I nodded, barely breathing.

Waving for me to follow, he went to change, no shower, unembarrassed in his nakedness, his white collared shirt clinging to the sweat on his back. I changed, too, keeping a low row of lockers between our waists, not daring to see or be seen.

He left without a backward glance, and I scrambled after him, marveling at the way he glowed in the cold, his reptilian musk, the awkward assurance of his imperfect swagger. An exiled god indeed, bound in a human form yet bright as the midnight sky. I wanted to be him then, so much more than I was with my small frame, my glasses, my limp hair, the smoothness of my skin and boy's belly, but I think I knew even then I never could be him, and so it was enough just to fall into his orbit.

We cut across the basketball courts to the lotus pond where all the students played between classes when the weather was sweet and warm, the place the teachers held court when they didn't want to teach, the place where two black swans spent their days swimming with the koi and waiting to fly.

We call them sky geese in Mandarin. It sounds silly in English, but the Mandarin is beautiful. First the crystalline chime of *tian*, high and pure as a cloudless blue sky and then the throaty waternote of the *e* rising up on ponderous wings. *Swan* sounds froggy and squat, but *tian'e* soars.

Some rich alumnus donated the ones at the school, a mated pair of onyx birds the superlative of any gaudy peacock, but their wings were clipped, and they lived bound to the water, tormented by children, forever hungry. I thought Omi was going to do something nasty, another cruel prank, and when he swung his backpack around and rummaged inside, I almost lost my nerve again. Then he pulled out a bag of *qingcai* and sank into a flat-footed squat on the edge of the pond while the swans and I warily watched.

"Come on," he said, "don't be a goose," and tossed a handful of leaves into the water just out of arm's reach. I squatted beside him. First one and then the other swan swam forward, webbed feet churning the jade water. They craned their reedy necks this way and that, fixing us with small, suspicious eyes the color of moss before pecking up the leaves.

Side by side, a mere foot between us, we watched them eat. Omi tossed in more leaves and passed me a handful, our fingertips not quite touching. The swans regarded us inscrutably when the last leaves were gone and then continued their peregrinations. Omi stood and I followed, too fast and too clumsy, startling the birds.

"You gotta take your time. Don't move so fast or you'll scare 'em away."

"Sorry," I said as the warning bell rang, and Omi beelined for the school. I took two skipping steps to fall in beside him, but he seemed to stay slightly ahead, sweeping me along in his wake.

"How long have you been feeding them?"

"Couple of weeks."

"Why?"

"Everyone's hungry, right?" He veered to the left. "I gotta pee. See ya."

"Bye," I said, but he was already beyond the bathroom curtains, and I was alone in the too-small hall raucous with little children.

That evening, I wheedled fifty *kuai* off my dad while he was drunk and distracted on the phone with someone from work. I chafed at the ignominy of my need, but once I had the money in hand, my first taste of moral compromise seemed less bitter.

After dinner I went down to the Lawson's to buy bread, the sort of sweet pastry so popular at Chinese convenience stores. On the way back, a smothering tightness overtook me in the way my shoes suddenly pinched my feet, the way my jacket strained against my shoulders, the way my skin prickled as I thought of Omi. When I got home, I asked in a fluster, "We're not gonna be late tomorrow, are we?"

"Same time as always," mom said, "What's the bread for?"

"Something at school."

She gave me a funny look and ruffled my hair.

"Stop!" I squawked, and she smiled, then sent me off to my homework where the ink from my pen, transmuted by some prurient alchemy, swelled into doodles of Omi, and by bedtime, I was ravenous for the dark. I laid on the duvet without my pajama top for the first time in memory, hands beneath my head, spreading my shoulders like wings. Moonlight the same ash-silver shade as Omi's skin came spilling like a Tang poem through the window, across the blankets, over my restless legs, brushing my belly and bare chest. My chin. My lower lip. The blades of my teeth.

The air turned frosty overnight, as if in jealousy or judgment, and Omi steamed in the cold as he walked from the gym towards the pond.

"Hey!" I called, running up, my backpack swinging stupidly. "Can I come with you?"

"Yep. Don't scare 'em this time though, *haoba*?"

I bobbled my head, and we squatted down by the water's edge, "Here," I said, keeping my voice low, unzipping my backpack with exaggerated care, and handing him the sweetbread.

Omi shook his head, "Not good for 'em."

My bones went noodly and my face flamed. Omi didn't seem to notice and began tearing leaves from the *qingcai*, ripping them off at the root and waggling them at the wary swans before tossing them into the water a hair's breadth closer than the day before. He passed some to me, and I followed his lead, shame forgotten.

For the rest of the week, we repeated the ritual, tossing the leaves almost within reach and drawing the swans closer. All the while, I inched closer to Omi until by Friday our knees almost touched. I was heady with the nearness, and my fledgling concupiscence fluttered all day long before falling to earth as I watched Omi return to the dorms from the car window. I spent the weekend moody and moping like Romeo pining for Rosaline, worried my parents might smell it on me, whatever this new scent was that stank of copper and salt and the yolky tang of my lust, and by Sunday night I was back to sleeping in all my PJs like a little boy, the curtains closed tight.

On Monday morning, I yanked my head away when mom reached out to pat my hair outside the school. Her hurt was instant and confused, like still-glowing darkness the moment a bulb burns out, but in her maternal wisdom she gave me a sad little smile and said *zaijian* as if it were the smallest goodbye in the world. My car door clicked closed with a whimper and I slunk my way through the gate.

I almost skipped meeting Omi, and when I finally gave in, I made a point to put a little distance between us as we walked to the pond from the gym. The swans were wary, too, after their treatless weekend, but as always Omi didn't seem to notice the tension in any of us and with a buddha's forbearance, he yielded the space, tossing the leaves far enough out into the pond that there was no danger of interaction. It worked, and by Wednesday desire conquered dread. While I contrived the best way to graze my knee against Omi's, the swans abandoned all caution to snatch the leaves straight from our fingers, gulping them down like dodos drinking from a crocodile wallow.

On Thursday, the swans ate from Omi's left hand while his right crept unseen through the brittle November air. One finger, delicate as spun sugar, brushed the back of the big swan's head. It flinched and honked, feathers bristling like cactus spines. Omi froze. They eyed one another, green-black to black-green. It snatched another leaf, shook its feathers slack, and Omi's finger fell into a soft slow stroke. He turned his round pale face to me and grinned as only the innocent can. It was the look of children in Christmas movies, of delight unblemished by age. The smaller swan followed the other and I followed Omi, stroking her head. We lingered briefly like first frost until all the leaves were gone and the bell rang.

I surrendered to myself that night and for the first time faced my parents fearlessly in the Friday morning glare. I put myself to within an atom's breadth of Omi, bold and hungry, and when he didn't move away, when I thought I felt his pulse arcing across the sliver of space between us, my heart soared like swans returned to flight. The birds cut sharp across the pond when they spotted us teetering on the edge and the wind-rippled water swelled in the rough wake of their passage. They ate greedily, right up against the concrete berm, their delicate throats brushing our knees. Just a little farther and I would know him at last. I let my leg go slack and tip towards Omi's.

I almost missed it when his fingers stiffened, clamping shut like jaws, and with one casual pop of his wrist he snapped the bird's neck. My leg recoiled and my bird jerked away, drawing blood from my fingertip, honking, puffing up her feathers, zipping back across the water in frightened, failed flight. Omi snatched at her almost playfully, beating the air, then barked an ugly laugh and said, "*Shabi*," as the bird made the safety of the deep water. He tossed the rest of the *qingcai* into the weeds, brushed his hands on his pants, and gave the dead bird a little push with his foot to set it bobbing after its partner, grinning the same grin from when he first touched those once-glossy feathers.

"Pretty stupid, huh?" he said as the bell rang, and he headed for the school. The principal and Omi's mom came for him in the middle of Mr. Joyce's class right as Friar Laurence was chirping warnings upon deaf ears. Omi tossed his book on the desk without a word and walked to the door where the pair lowered, stiff-necked and black-clad like avian ghosts, his shoulder clipping mine on the way out.

DANIEL MONZINGO *teaches high school literature and is a student in the University of Texas El Paso's bilingual online MFA program. Originally from East Texas, he now lives in Shanghai, China, with his spouse and their many pets. "The Swans" is his first publication.*

Going Again
Will James Limón

The end of March always brings up the same memory of my grandfather, as if spring can't truly begin without it. 1969. The clanging telephone woke me up. The night before, I'd fallen asleep in the living room watching TV, a sixteen-year-old trying to drown out the creaks and groans of an empty house, abandoned for the weekend by parents needing to see my older sister in L.A. "Damn drug difficulties," Dad had growled. They told me not to have anyone over and not to drive the car except in an emergency. "Be the good child," Mom had said softly and closed up her suitcase while Dad had muttered, "And goddammit, stay home." I jerked my face off the damp sofa cushion and picked up the phone. "Hello?"

A thick voice crackled through. "I need Jimmy, *ja*? Jimmy *ist das* you?"

"What?"

"It *ist* Jimmy. *Gute morgen!*"

"Gramps?" I sat up.

"*Ja*. You 'wake?"

"Yes, I mean *ja*, Gramps. I'm awake. Sort of."

"*Gut. Und* you should be awake. Fine *morgen*, fine *tag*-day."

Gramps had never called just to talk to me. He was ninety-one years old and lived on the other side of San Diego but might as well have been in Germany for all I ever saw of him. He and Dad didn't get along. Something about money. Once, Mom had complained about wanting to have Gramps over, but Dad just waved his hand and said, "Enough." I hadn't seen him for over a year. It'd been almost seventy-five years since he sailed to America, yet his German accent remained strong, his voice gravelly, and I always found it funny how he mixed languages.

"Jimmy?"

"*Ja*, Gramps?"

"Have *schule*?"

"No, it's Saturday."

"Gut. Today, you *hier* are needed.

"Anything wrong?"

"*Nein. Komm.* I will make *gut speise*, bratwurst on thick rye bread. Keep you strong."

This surprised me. In my whole life he'd never made a meal for anyone in our family. After working in a greasy little restaurant for almost sixty years, I figured Gramps never wanted to cook for anyone again.

"Mom and Dad went to see Chrissy in L.A. They don't want me to drive anywhere unless it's an emergency. They don't trust me." I didn't want to tell him that I'd never driven all the way across the city and had only been on the freeway three times by myself.

He coughed suddenly, a deep gouging gasp that sent pops of phlegm rattling up from his lungs.

"Sure you're all right?"

"*Ja*," his voice grated into the phone. "I *sprach mit* your *mutter* yesterday and your sister the *tag*-day before that. Now you I must see." He coughed once more and said in a whisper, "*Komm, meiner wunderbar junge.* Just *komm. Sehr* important."

You I must see stayed in my head while I ate a bowl of cereal and showered. If there wasn't a problem, what did he need me for? I had a half-built '55 Chevy model and some homework to finish, and no one was there to tell me what to do. I felt scared to drive so far alone and worried that I'd get in trouble. But Gramps was old, and that cough sounded really bad. Maybe it *was* an emergency.

When I pulled up, I saw his face behind the front window of the apartment. By the time I got out of the Ford, he stood in the open doorway, wearing a long-sleeved button-up white shirt and black suspenders attached to black dress pants. Three inches shorter than me, he stood ramrod straight, a fringe of snow-white hair surrounding his smooth bald head. His full white beard cascaded along each cheek, around his mouth, and over his chin to below his belt buckle. He'd always reminded me of a miniature Santa Claus. His wire-rimmed reading glasses completed the picture. The beard was his trademark. No one had ever seen him without it, not even my mother. He'd stroke it as if petting a white cat and did so now as he smiled at me, reddish lips peeking out from within the white whiskers like two curled rose petals stuck in the snow.

"Hi Gramps. What's the occasion?"

His face followed the aim of my eyes traveling down to his shiny patent leather shoes. "Company *kommst*, I dress the part." He surprised me with a quick hug, his whiskers warming my cheek. Then, he moved to one side and motioned me to enter, his hand placed gently on my back. "*Sitz.*" He steered me to the blue cloth recliner and sat next to me on the old leather couch that had been there forever, its mottled brown leather worn to a soft shine much like the back of his hands. Gramps's apartment always smelled the same—a sour aroma of stale sweat, old skin, and dusty books.

"So, how do you like *hoch schule*-school, being on your own this weekend, all grown up acting?"

"It's okay."

"*Ja, nicht wahr?*" He cocked his head to one side like an old parrot. "Got girl?"

"No, not yet." I felt my face warm.

"*Das ist gut, sehr gut. Junge* like you doesn't need to get all tied down. Later, time for that." He looked away for a few moments, and I was surprised to see his eyes tear up. He took a thin, yellowed handkerchief out of a back pocket and blew his nose, making a loud snort, and wiped his nostrils. I remember thinking he must have allergies or something, although I'd never seen him this way before.

On the bookcase behind Gramps sat the antique tabletop grandfather's clock, its pendulum swinging time away with the ominous swish-click I'd heard over the years. It reminded me of when Chrissy and I had stayed with him while Mom remained in the hospital after her operation and Dad had to work. I was seven. Gramps lay me down on the leather couch to take a nap. "*Schlaf gut*," he whispered. I couldn't. The ticking kept me awake. Too frightened to say anything, I had stayed as still as possible, pretending I was dead, keeping my eyes closed for what had seemed like hours. You don't hear clocks like that anymore.

"What's up?" I asked, hoping Mom wouldn't call home while I was gone. She'd go crazy if she knew I'd driven here by myself. Dad would just get pissed.

Gramps stared at me, his lower lip quivering slightly. "*Komm mit mier.*" I followed him into the tiny kitchen packed with its old, white refrigerator and a chrome-legged fake marble table surrounded by four plastic peeling gray leatherette chairs. On the table sat a small white porcelain basin. Next to it were two scissors, a metal safety razor with a pack of blades, a can of shaving cream, and a small oval mirror with a wooden handle. He motioned me to the chair by the window. "*Sitz.*" As I did so, he sat down next to me, the daylight illuminating his beard. "I want *mein* face cleaned off." He smiled and his beard widened slightly, changing his appearance to an aged Merlin without the wizard's coned hat.

"What?" I thought he wanted me to shampoo his beard or something, but there was no soap on the table other than the shaving cream, and the basin was empty.

He tugged at the bottom of his beard. "Take my whiskers off, *vollstandig*-complete."

"You want me to shave off your beard?"

"*Ja.*" My face must have shown my amazement because his smile turned into a hearty laugh.

"I don't understand. Without your beard, you wouldn't be Gramps," I blurted, sounding like a six-year-old.

He laughed louder, pulled out his handkerchief once more and wiped his eyes. "*Nichts* to worry, *junge*." He reached over and patted my cheek, his wrinkled fingers feeling rough. "Time for a change," he said softly. "Time to be young again."

Gramps young? Again? I tried to imagine his Santa Claus face clean shaven, feeling as anxious and excited as I had during my first solo in the Ford three months ago when Mom sent me five blocks to the Safeway to bring back a dozen eggs. But driver's training had taught me what to do. I'd only shaved three times in my life and then with an electric razor. The only safety razors I'd ever seen were those hanging in the store. "Gramps? Can't you just do it?" My voice sounded very small.

"*Nein*. I want to feel it, not see it. You must cut."

"Don't you have an electric razor? Can't we get one?" I pointed at the razor and package of blades. "I mean, these things—I don't know."

Then he said something that made no sense. "*Nicht genug zeit*. Not enough time." His voice became very low. "Lessons today, Jimmy. For us both." He touched my hand. "I will teach. No worry." Then, without another word, he produced an old black-and-white photograph, yellowed and crumbly at the edges. In it, a short man stood next to a tall horse. The horse had moved slightly, blurring its image, but the young man was in focus: stern, stiffly posed, black eyes staring directly out at you from the past as if he owned all of time. He wore his dark hair combed down across his forehead and closely cropped on the sides. In his hand he held a bowler hat and the vest of his three-piece suit was buttoned all the way to the top.

"Me," Gramps said. "I was *vier-und-zwanzig*, twenty-four, living in New York City. 1902, seven years after I came to America."

The young man didn't resemble Gramps at all—much younger of course, no beard, dark hair on his head. But when I examined his face more closely, I noticed the same little droop in the right eyelid. It was Gramps all right. Only eight years older than me.

"Gosh," I said softly, wondering if I'd ever get to be ninety-one and see a photo of a young me, and if I'd look that different.

He chuckled. "*Ja*, gosh. *Ja. Erste*-first, *junge*," he took my right hand, placed it over the large scissors on the table and motioned to his face. "Cut the big *haar*. Step by step we'll take it."

I scooted my chair closer and picked up the scissors, remembering a story Mom had told me a few years before. As a little girl of five, she had sneaked up on Gramps while he took a nap and snipped off a tuft of his beard with a nail trimmer. He'd roared up, outraged at the tiny bald spot on his cheek, scaring her to tears. "That beard is just like him, tough, wiry, and not to be fooled with," she told me. Standing behind Mom, Dad had added, "A-fucking-men," rolling his eyes in his "what-a-nut" expression I knew so well. Now, Gramps wanted me to cut it off?

He leaned back in the chair and closed his eyes, just the hint of a smile on his lips. I moved closer with the scissors, slowing as I approached his face until I hovered over him, reluctant to put the blades around his beard.

"Cut," he said. "Begin at bottom."

I reached down, slowly slid my hand underneath the beard and lifted the silvery hair off his chest. It felt fine but strong—wiry. I opened the scissors and pushed the blades into the hair. Squeezed the handles. At first, I felt resistance then came a crunch as the scissors sliced through the beard. Gramps flinched. I stopped.

"Go on."

I cut five inches off the bottom of the beard and put the hair in the pan. He looked different already. With it cut straight across, he'd changed from Santa Claus to a leprechaun. I started to laugh.

His eyes popped open. "*Was*-what?" He glanced down at his chest, then picked up the mirror, looked into it and started laughing, too. "Straight *mann*, eh?" We laughed together, leaning into each other, almost bumping heads. The oily, sweaty smell from before now grew into a husky musk. "*Fortsetzt*," he said, wiping his eyes with his hand and settling back into position with eyes closed. "Continue."

I cut the side off at an angle so that the shortened beard was now much longer on the right than on the left. I started chuckling again.

He checked the mirror and let out a belly laugh like an old car horn. We both roared even louder until he started coughing. And it seemed like he couldn't stop.

"Grandpa, shouldn't you see a doctor?"

He held up his hand, shaking violently until he calmed down, took out his handkerchief and spit something red into it. "*Wasser, bitte*-please," he rasped. I got him a glass and he drank it, sputtering between coughs. Finally, he breathed normally. "*Nicht* worry," he said, quickly wadding up the handkerchief and stuffing it into his pocket. But his smile was gone. "*Bitte.*" He motioned for me to proceed.

Slowly, I trimmed the beard as close to his face as I dared. "Now, use the little one," he said without opening his eyes. "I will be still as a picture." And he was, not moving a muscle while I cut and trimmed, putting the smaller tufts of snow-white hair into the basin with the rest of it. Finally, I reached the limit of what could be done even with the little scissors. Before me was an entirely different man. I could see the outlines of his jaw which were more square than I would have guessed, and his cheeks puffed out slightly as he breathed. Even though my efforts had left the remaining beard uneven, he looked years younger yet still distinguished, a Santa changed to leprechaun changed to what looked like the picture of Tchaikovsky.

He opened his eyes and aimed them at me. "So far *ist gut?*"

"I think so."

He picked up the mirror and examined his face, turning his head from side to side. "*Hungrig?*"

The wall clock said I'd been gone two hours already. "Yeah, sort of."

"Well, I am 'sort of' *hungrig* too. Let's eat. Give you strength to scratch off the rest of this old *haar.*"

Gramps got up and dusted stray hairs from his shirt into the sink. He picked up the basin and after a moment's hesitation, dumped the white beard hairs into the plastic trash bin by the back door. "No more a part of me," he muttered.

I moved the scissors, shaver, and shaving cream to one side as he placed a loaf of dark rye bread on a cutting board on the table. He took a half-eaten roll of bratwurst out of the refrigerator along with a jar of mayonnaise. "I would give you a beer, but you have to drive home afterwards," he said with a wink.

Gramps opened a drawer, pulled out a large knife, and cut the bread with quick strokes, making four thick slices that he handed to me, two on a plate. "Take a butter knife and spread on mayonnaise. Do not skimp." As I did so, he brought out a can of frozen lemonade and a bag of potato chips. That struck me as funny. I never really thought of Gramps eating potato chips.

"Let me tell you," he said, slicing the bratwurst into thin strips. "Sixteen, your age, to me this happened. I left the old country this way. Your mother does not know all this, but you will. *Hör mir zu*-Listen to me."

As we ate, Gramps told me how he'd grown up on a farm in eastern Germany. One summer afternoon he'd come in from the fields to news that both his parents and little sister had been killed in a buggy accident. Spooked by a snake, the horses ran wildly down a hill and slammed the buggy into a big oak tree. Three days after the funeral, his mother's brother, a huge man "with no *haar* and large teeth" raised a pistol toward him, saying he had ten minutes to gather his things and get off the property. Gramps grabbed some clothes and stuffed them into an old suitcase. While the uncle and aunt were out of the room, he had snatched a cooked chicken from the stove and put it in a basket. All this he told me in a flat tone without a hint of emotion.

"Then," he said, "I needed to be gone from that country. In those days, all young men had to be military. Those who refused were put in prison. That land I did not want to serve. I aimed to go to America to relatives. But I had no money, no ticket, *nichts*-nothing." Here, he raised his white eyebrows, wrinkling his forehead, and through his stubbly beard there were creases on his face I'd not seen before. "Only a plan I had." He tapped his head. "Oh, what a plan!" He told me he had stolen some of his aunt's clothes, dressed like a woman, and waited at the train station with his suitcase and the chicken in the basket. "They always let men board first, then women. As girl, had better chance to sneak on. Had not begun to shave yet, *junge*. Wearing those puffy women's clothes made me a homely *fräulein*, I am sure." He chortled, and I couldn't help laughing too, imagining Gramps as an ugly teenage girl.

"I was five the last time Chrissy dressed me in her clothes," I said. "Couldn't wait to get them off."

"Ach, *junge*," he said, his silver eyebrows drawn down. "This was serious business. If they had caught me—jail." He held his hands up with fingers curled as if gripping bars.

Gramps described how the men had worked their way through the gate and boarded the train. Then the women's line began to move. When he reached the front and the gatekeeper asked to see a ticket, Gramps pretended it was stuck in the valise. While he pretended to struggle to get it open, the whistle blew several times, and the train engine rumbled louder, belching steam and smoke. The women standing behind him in line worried that they'd miss the train and began to yell, "*Bewegen! Begwegen Sie dumm langsam madchen*. Move! Mooove, you slow, dumb girl," Gramps mimicked in a high-pitched voice, standing up, and waving his arms about. I crumpled over in laughter, spitting crumbs from the sandwich out of my mouth. He watched me, his eyes crinkly-bright, lips trembling. After making excuses and fumbling with the suitcase for several minutes, one huge old lady had shoved him forward beyond the entrance so she could get through. The crowd of women pushing at the gate had made it impossible for the gatekeeper to stop Gramps from boarding. "I ate that chicken on the train," he said, placing his hands on his stomach. "It was still *warm*."

Then, he leaned forward and cocked his head. "Jimmy, remember. There's a way out when you want it badly enough. Always."

I nodded.

After lunch we cleared the dishes. Gramps rinsed out the basin and filled it with hot tap water. Then, he opened the pack of razor blades, took one out and put it in the safety razor before screwing down its top. He held it up. "It's been sixty years since I shaved," he said. "A straight razor was used. With this thing, you and I are about as skilled." He winked at me. "All you have to do is slowly drag it along my skin. Do not worry. I can take a few nicks."

"I don't want to hurt you, Gramps. You sure we can't we get an electric one?"

"*Nein*. This will do. Go slowly, evenly." He wet his whiskers, squirted the shaving cream into his hands, and lathered both his face and neck. The pointed little peaks and swooping valleys in the foaming soap reminded me of the icing on my cousin's wedding cake last summer. Then he sat, closing his eyes and motioned me to begin. "Start at the top of the cheek at the middle of *mein* ear. Use even pressure." He pointed at the basin on the table. "Rinse off the soap *hier*."

I leaned over him. The razor trembled in my hand, and I reached over to steady myself on the back of Gramps' chair. Using scissors, it had been fun. But this was different, more dangerous. As I put the razor to his face, he twisted his jaw to make the skin taut. I pushed the razor into the foam until it touched his skin and pulled it down about two inches. It glided through the shaving cream and pushed a blob of soap onto the side of his face. I looked at the razor. Only shaving cream. "It's not working."

"Rinse off. More pressure. You will see."

I swished the razor in the water, the ball of shaving cream floated off like a tiny white island. This time I put the razor to his cheek and pulled down with more force, and I could feel the blade cut the whiskers. It sounded like fingernails drawn over sandpaper. Beneath my stroke, the pallid skin on his cheek appeared, something no one had seen in many years. "Got it," I whispered.

"*Gut*," he said and sighed. He sat back, relaxed, smiling as if recalling some private memory. "Around the jaw, be careful. Flat parts first. You'll learn."

Cautiously, I scraped off the left cheek. As I shaved the right side, the thin, raised welt of a scar appeared, red against his pale skin, running along the cheek about two inches above his jaw.

"Gently," he said, and I took extra care shaving the odd-angled whiskers that grew out of it.

By the time both cheeks were finished, I had the hang of it. I shaved under his nose, then along the jaw line and down his neck where, overconfident, I nicked him. "Oh, Gramps. I'm so sorry." A bead of red blood stained the white lather. I was horrified at the spreading pink spot in the shaving cream yet also fascinated by the bright color rising from such old, white skin.

He pointed to the table. "That little white stick there, rub it on the cut. That will stop the bleeding." When it did, I felt so relieved. "You are doing a good job, Jimmy. *Fabelhaft*-fabulous. I can tell. Maybe a barber you can be."

The furrows in his neck were more of a challenge, and the white stick saved me two more times. Gramps flinched only once and immediately reassured me. "You are doing all the *werk*," he said softly.

When I finished, his face was still smeared with a soapy film from the shaving cream, but it had no more whiskers on it. I stepped back and examined him. With the length of beard gone it seemed like he'd lost half his face. He did look younger than before, more like the man standing by the horse in the old photograph. But his wrinkled skin looked as white as the inside of a fish, and his shrunken cheeks made him seem more fragile. The scar gave him a rakish air that wasn't like the Gramps I'd always known. I got a funny feeling in my stomach.

He opened his eyes and grinned. "Who you expected?"

"I don't know. I guess."

He stood slowly, went to the sink, leaned over, and rinsed off his face, patting his cheeks gently with the water. When finished, he tore off two sheets from the paper towel roll and gently dabbed it dry. He straightened up and stroked his face. "Smooth, *nicht wahr?*"

"Very smooth."

Gramps walked to the table, picked up the mirror and looked into its glass with unblinking eyes, stroking his face with the palm of his hand. He ran one finger along the scar. "*Sehr seltsam*-very strange." Then, under his breath, he muttered, "*Welkommen, welkommen*," and I thought I saw sadness in his eyes. He turned to me. "*Vortrefflich, junge*, excellent job. I am proud of you. I salute you." He stood straight and raised his angled right hand to his brow. "Now, *sitz*. I have something else to show you."

He left the kitchen and returned with another old black-and-white photograph. This one was bigger. Like the first picture, he had no beard and no scar, but here he wasn't as young. Next to him stood a short woman, very pretty with high cheekbones and shining eyes. Both were dressed formally, standing stiff, unsmiling. She wore a large hat; he was bareheaded. Her arm threaded through his. "My wife," he said softly.

"Grandma?

"No. First wife."

That shocked me into silence. I never knew he'd been married before Grandma.

His finger lingered on the surface of the photo, tracing the outline of her face. "I was thirty-one; she twenty-two." He paused. "Day after this taken, a man with a knife attacked us on the street. I got this but couldn't save her." I looked up at him. His fingers touched the scar, but his glistening eyes stayed on the photo. "Poor Talia." His mouth twitched and he sighed, a long slow breath. "Never I shaved again."

I didn't know what to say. Still don't. If Gramps were here today I'd be as silent as I was at sixteen, sitting in his kitchen, seeing a photo of a wife who'd been murdered and knowing that if she'd lived I would never have been born. I felt heavy in the chair. Stinging prickled my eyes. I kept blinking until I could see the picture better.

"My face I wanted to hide. My shame. Went away where no one knew me." He stopped. I kept my eyes on her. "Longer my beard grew, longer and longer." He sighed again, air seeping out from his lungs. "Came to California. Time went by. I started cooking in Louie's restaurant, married your grandma, had kids, was happy."

He didn't sound happy. His fingertip circled the woman's face on the picture. Finally, he stopped and whispered, "Jimmy?"

"Yes, Gramps?"

"Look at me, Jimmy."

I didn't want to. I felt afraid of what he might look like with his new face and sad voice, and a woman who'd been his wife murdered in front of him.

"Jimmy, *mein schöner*-beautiful *junge*. Look."

I did. He put both hands on my shoulders. Even though I was sitting, his head wasn't much higher than mine. He stared straight into my eyes, his right eyelid with that little droop. The light glinted off the skin of his face, and the scar gleamed a crimson line across his cheek. "Never hide. Do what you do in your life. *Gott* knows, do the best you can. But whatever happens, never hide. Not once, not never. *Versteht?* Understand?" Eyes moist, his lips quivered as if he were going to say more, but he made no sound. I didn't know what to do except nod and hold his gaze, smelling the bratwurst on his breath. Time paused with a stillness unlike any other moment I have ever known. He closed his eyes. Then, he slapped both of my shoulders with his hands and turned away, coughing. "*Samstag*-Saturday. Going fast. Better get home," he said, his voice husky.

"Yeah. Mom might call and be worried if I don't answer." I took a deep breath. I didn't want to go.

"*Eine minute, bitte*-please." Gramps disappeared into the living room. He came shambling back with his right hand closed into a fist. "Something for you. My thanks for your help today." He presented the fist, nodding at me to touch it. When I did, he opened it to reveal an old pocket watch, a Waltham, with a thick leather strap attached to a miniature horseshoe. It was ticking and told the correct time. "Old watch from the Old World. It works. Not many things that old still do." He smiled slightly and cleared his throat. "See?" We looked at the photograph of him standing by the horse. Sure enough, there was the little silver horseshoe, dangling from his pocket. I held the watch with both hands. It ticked loudly, its bold black hands poised above the faded white face. "I used it many years, many. Part of my youth. Now, part of yours."

I glanced up at him, and he was beaming differently than before. No longer Santa Claus or a leprechaun or a stranger. He was my grandfather again, both old and new, and very tired. I smiled "Thank you, Gramps. This was a fun day." What else does a sixteen-year-old say?

He nodded again, then coughed violently for almost a minute, and this time the water I brought him didn't help right away.

"Sorry," he said finally.

"Are you going to be okay?"

"*Ja, ja.*"

I wanted to believe him. I'm not sure I did.

At the door, he handed me an envelope. "These are just for you to keep." Then, he hugged me close for a longer time than he'd ever done before. No whiskers tickled my face, just his smooth, worn cheek. Warm, so warm. "All we shared today for you. No one else," he whispered into my ear. "It's our *speziell* secret. Just you and me."

"Okay," I whispered back.

He stood at the window as I drove away and waved until he put his hand to his mouth to cough.

I opened the envelope after I got home. Inside were the two photographs he'd shown me—Gramps as a young man and the one with his first wife. Each March I pull them out and gaze into those distant eyes, so alive in the faded sunlight. It's funny how they look younger as time goes by.

My grandfather passed away in his sleep later that weekend. At his funeral, the coffin was closed. I didn't ask why. Mom never said anything about how different he looked. She only told us that she'd put in the casket two items she found in his apartment—her mother's faded wedding dress and, in a tiny, etched-glass box, a dried-up sliver of white wedding cake.

All these years, I've wondered which marriage the cake came from.

WILL JAMES LIMÓN *is an educator, counselor, and author of several nonfiction books. His publishers include HarperCollins, Hazelden, New Harbinger Publications, Inc., and Wilhelm Heyne Verlag in Germany. "Young Again", the short story included in* The Masters Review Anthology XII, *is his first fiction publication. His fiction interests range from picture books and middle-grade to adult short stories and novels. An avid horn player and pianist, he also composes classical music. He lives with his wife at 8,500 feet in the mountains of Colorado.*

An Afternoon at the Edge of the World

Jenny Hayden Halper

In eight years, when my mother doesn't have much time left and is trying to convince me she did the best she could, she will tell me she picked reform school because of a long list of non-threatenings. My mother makes adjectives nouns; you'd never know she worked in magazines.

Non-threatenings: no families to screw you up, no boys to distract you, no drugs to distract you, no stores to steal from, extremely limited screen time, a man-made waterfall, a heated swimming pool, everything—even the gardens, even the flowers—exactly the same. There's a lake and a river but they're both fake. When I ask why she sent me here, she writes, "You needed to shape up, Grace." It is up to me to fill in the blanks.

I let her fill in blanks too: the school is fine and my friends are fine and all girls is fine and baseball—really softball, which she doesn't approve of—is fine. In real life I hit the most hits, underhand pitch the most strikes, but over email I don't remember the scores of anything. The food is fine.

"How are your classes?"

"How is your dorm?"

"How is your figure?"
Fine.

"That word is a curse," my mother writes, sitting in our Upper East Side apartment or on a leather chair in Lewis's Upper West Side apartment, picking at the tip of her French manicure. Or getting a French manicure; Lewis is the kind of guy who has people come to the house.

I'd tell her to come visit me if she wants me to stop saying "Fine" but she's already answered that question: she doesn't drive.

I am fifteen years and two days old. My mother has missed my birthday, and when I write her an email telling her about the day's events—the dining hall singing to me, my softball coach/English teacher/homeroom teacher, Iris, bringing a cake to practice, a home run when I was barely looking at the ball, my temporary best friend Madeline sneaking her brother into our dorm room, leaving us alone in the dark—I make sure everything sounds better than a spa day or a diner at midnight. This is the best birthday I've had, ever. This is the best birthday even though she wasn't there.

I don't tell her that the ground is so dry dust lives under our fingernails. The knees of my jeans are permanently brown. I especially don't tell her that the sinks and toilets are cut off in the middle of the night so the flow of water—underground pipes pumping up the waterfall—won't dry out. I tell her Madeline's brother is adopted and French, a potential *Look Mom I can make adjectives nouns too.*

She doesn't write back.

I google her new column, "How to Make Time," an aqua backdrop and curved fonts, a development post-Lewis. I write "I want to come home" in the comments section, but she doesn't respond to that.

* * *

My mother met Lewis outside the Goldman Sachs building, where he used to work before he realized he could make more on his own. It wasn't his money—my mother always dated rich men. What impressed her was that he could hail a taxi in two seconds flat. On their first date he decided everything—where they would go, what they would eat, what time his driver would drop her back at her apartment, how long he would have to stand outside our window until she squeezed onto the fire escape and blew a kiss back.

"He has invisible power," she told me, sitting on the toilet seat, knees pulled into her chest, chewing gummy vitamins. "This is the one, Grace, I'm telling you." She liked to have conversations while I was in the shower, which meant I had to be careful to hide the tattoo my friend's uncle had given me in Chinatown. Right above my butt—a silk moth, a symbol of prosperity and reincarnation, but all my mother would see was ink and blood.

I should explain that my mother is not one of those typical self-help magazine women, a breed generally marked by rubbery, processed skin and hair that's been dyed into breakable straw. She actually uses cucumbers on her eyes, eats the brain-restoring meals she recommends, stays away from chemicals, thinks "How do I want to look when I'm sixty?" not "How do I want to look tomorrow?" As a result, she looks like the women her readers aspire to. Even if I wasn't her daughter, I would say she's very beautiful.

Before Lewis we lived in a one-bedroom apartment on the Upper East Side. I got the bedroom; she slept on the pull-out couch. I'd wake up and she'd be sitting at the kitchen table in a tank top, black curls clipped back, flipping between profiles on millionairematch.com, flirting with men she'd never meet. I'd swirl a spoon into the Activia yogurt. She would say it tasted like a chemical bath.

"Have you tasted it?"

"I can smell it," my mother said. She'd recently done a print piece on how to save the planet and your skin simultaneously by using fruit compost as a toiletry. She'd asked me for feedback. I was fourteen and wouldn't go anywhere near a spa. My mother waited patiently, sipped her mug of wine—wine before breakfast, which has been her habit my entire life.

"How was your latest?" I would ask, and she listed qualities she admired about the men she dated, qualities she knew would inevitably rot or go wrong. The morning after her first date with Lewis she was out on the fire escape when I finished getting dressed for school. Her robe was tied tight, her chin tilted up towards a May rain cloud. The air was thick and warm, but she was shivering.

"How was your latest?" I asked, sitting on the windowsill, and she said nothing, and it was as close as she'd gotten, ever, to telling me not to call him that.

* * *

When I get scared, which is often, especially when Iris threatens solitary confinement, this is what I do—I remind myself my mother almost witnessed the end of the world. This happened in Illinois when she was almost twelve. My mother's father was a meteorologist who predicted Lake Michigan would dip way below normal levels and possibly evaporate. The world was using up too much energy, he said, technology would be the death of all of us.

He sent an email to exactly five cousins, his brother, two friends. He told them to stock up on canned foods, water bottles, even gasoline before it was too late. My mother wasn't allowed to tell anyone else. It was summer and he took her to work with him so she'd see there were things to care about besides red lip gloss, ballet flats, shining a flashlight across the street at her friend Damien's window every night.

My mother was smart and now she had a secret and these were things that came with responsibility. She sat in her father's observatory and they watched the water level drop. Soon Lake Michigan was full of rotting fish; cats were curling up under limp flowers and putting themselves to sleep. Damien—the salient detail she provided was that he was fat—kept having dreams about walking off the edge of the world into pitch black nothing. He had this idea that they would find the end of the drought, the spot where water was still knee height, they would figure out what was different and replicate it. Damien said they could save everyone.

One day, my mother told me, they walked to Lake Michigan and kept on walking. They walked so far their ankles ached and the sky got dark and they ran out of the fruit and nuts Damien had packed. The almost-empty lake, it wouldn't end. It went on struggling forever. A pair of fish flopped in front of them and died. Damien sat down on the ground and started crying and my mother realized he'd never be strong enough to protect her. She thought she loved him, and since she was young enough to still be honest, she was probably right.

You need to keep your goals simple, my mother writes at the beginning of her column. *How to Make Time: The Essentials.* There's an airbrushed picture that makes her look less special—her nose is narrow and her eyes are vacant, too blue. Her face fills the top half of the screen and of course I scroll down and read her tips: make lists, set attainable goals, pamper yourself (healthfully), don't let others bog you down with their problems, meditate, do one thing every day that scares you, start with that as number one.

* * *

The campus is pitch black after midnight. The dorms are in these giant farm houses, the sound of breathing travels through the walls. I am easily spooked. This is a thing I am working on getting over. Lewis, who sent me here, says this place in particular, and reform schools in general, are about self-improvement. I open the window and I flatten my stomach and soon I'm out on a thick branch of the tree Madeline and I have been climbing. Soon I'm all alone in the dark, my heart up in my forehead. I can't breathe either, that's how scared I am.

In reform school, everything is temperature controlled. The flowers are planted by machines that look like tractors and are stored behind the parking lot. I smoke a clove cigarette from Madeleine's non-biological French brother. The waterfall pours muddy blue water into the wide part of the river, built by a team of conservationists maybe fifteen years ago. So the waterfall is my age. "How do you build a waterfall?" I've asked Iris, on more than one occasion, when the softball team is picnicking down here, but she responds to questions she doesn't know the answer to by telling me to go on Google.

The next morning Madeline closes the window and says we have to be careful because Iris and her spy (her twelve-year-old son, Jerome), have been lurking around, and if you're caught outside that's grounds for calling parents and solitary confinement. I make a note to do it more often. Madeline's red hair is in two puffy braids because she slept that way.

"We have to be careful," she says, "but it would be great to have stalkers."

Sometimes I agree with her and sometimes I don't. During softball practice, Iris's son hangs near the field, pretending to do his homework but probably gathering cigarette butts, hair flopping over his eyes.

"Jerome, you're making me nervous," Iris calls. "The brain is not a replaceable object. Stay in the dugout, or go to the car."

Iris lobs easy pitches, and I hit them, one after the other, but they go right to Iris, right to her glove. After practice, Jerome trails behind her, his small hands effortlessly hauling aluminum bats into Iris's threadbare bag. Together they gather the whole field, even the bases and home plate, which need constant cleaning. When they have finished, they gulp from plastic bottles. Chin still tilted back, still drinking, she gives his head a little squeeze, as though it is a precious thing.

*　*　*

I've always told my friends my mother's origins are secret. Her life before me is a blank slate—no grandparents, no aunts and uncles, no pictures, nothing. After my mother met Lewis, she never mentioned the drought or any memories from childhood. He liked to think she came out fully formed and beautiful, forever thirty-five. Her voice had a clearer, sharper, crystal quality. I wondered if he brainwashed her, made her forget anything bad had ever happened. *How to Make Time for Happiness*, she wrote, *How to Make Time for Love.*

The night I met Lewis for the first time my mother shoved me into a uniform from the Catholic School I went to for a year. I was nervous, and my feet itched, and I felt like I was going to pop out of my skirt.

"Are you good?" my mother asked. She had this wide-eyed look resembling concern and for a moment I allowed myself to think she really was. Our taxi dipped into a tunnel. She was wearing white suede gloves. She'd been wearing them a lot, lately. It was June.

"As long as he feeds me, I'm fine," I said, and she put one of the gloves on my knee and it stayed there, uncomfortable.

"Good, then," she said, and I said, "Tell me about the drought," hoping she'd get to the part when she and Damien tried to save the world. My mother's sharp cheekbones caught light from the street lamps. "Grace, my love," she said, "you're a little old for that one, don't you think?"

Lewis's building was marble floors and huge glass windows. There were not two doormen but four; they wore zipped-up satin outfits and whistles around their necks. Lewis didn't answer the door, a butler did, a round, unfailingly polite Black man with, my mother noted, a Rolex, the thousand-dollar kind. The elevator opened into a cream-colored living room with a couch shaped like a horseshoe and two fireplaces reflecting flames. We waited there staring at empty wine glasses and a bowl of salted peanuts.

"Take a look outside," my mother said. His balcony was big and stone, nothing like our fire escape with its sliver view of the East River.

"Grace," my mother said, "come back here." Her voice had that new cut crystal quality. If I'd listened closely, I would have noticed it was also very tired. She said my name again, loudly. I thought, in that moment, that she had named me what she wanted me to be. Then she actually giggled.

Lewis wore cycling clothes—spandex shorts, a red t-shirt that said *Stanford*, a helmet tucked under his arm. He probably does coke, I remember thinking. I remember making a mental note to do a search of the apartment. He had a separate room for his bicycles. It was the size of our entire apartment, and smelled of nail polish and rubber. Lewis fed us snails he said were shipped from the south of France. There was a helicopter specially designated to bring food from his favorite countries, Lewis explained, more for my mother's benefit than for mine.

* * *

At the end of every term, Iris has to do a report about our progress, our grades, our ability to work as a team (hence the softball), even our physical health. Madeleine says that's why she's such a bitch sometimes. I don't think she's a bitch but I don't like her either. I haven't stopped going out at night to watch the waterfall with store-bought goldfish in it, and the week after my birthday I start sneaking into the computer lab at night, reading my mother's column: *How to Make Time for Proper Nutrition*, *How to Make Time for Exercise*, *How to Make Time for Sex*.

One night I even fall asleep in front of the computer, that stupid airbrushed picture of my mother staring down at me, and when I wake up the sun is peeking orange through the windows, and my ear has typed a string of letters: *Rrguazqqazqqzaqqaq*, into her comments, and my mother has already responded, *Dear reader, I don't understand what you wrote*.

Iris says she knows who has been in the computer lab, and if they don't stop there are going to be consequences. She doesn't look at me. I'm pitching today and I can see Jerome at the edge of the field, pretending to scribble answers in a notebook. Really, though, he's watching me and he's watching Iris and every time my pitch gets hit she throws her hands up and stalks in an explosive circle and when the least athletic player hits a home run she screams out "You are absolutely useless," and later Madeline, who is devoted to me for some reason, says, "I can have my brother beat her up if you want."

"That's really okay."

"It's verbal abuse, you should report it to the school board."

Iris is, basically, the school board; her funders are people like Lewis, rich and extremely oblivious for smart people.

"It's really okay."

Later that afternoon, when I've slept through English and woken when the classroom is empty, Iris comes over, puts her hand on my shoulder. She says, "You think you're special but you're not."

Reform school is supposed to love you into goodness. Madeline says she's seen this work, kids who should have been in prison suddenly acing math tests and writing papers on Thoreau in French. Reform school is genetically engineered sunflowers that would drive my mother mad, Wonder Bread with fiber, leaves that turn orange at the same time, a too-bright corner of a baseball diamond with the goal of team spirit and cooperation, not on continuing America's favorite pastime. Iris is trying to break me.

"You're not looking at the fucking ball," she says now, or maybe she doesn't say "fucking" but it comes out that way, sharp and with an imaginary wad of spit. "I'm benching you, Grace, if you strike out again." And then Linda's lobbing them, baby-easy, over home plate.

I give up and leave the baseball diamond for the weeds and sit next to Jerome who is filling his math sheet with gleeful cartoon animals, these strange anime-like creatures with question marks for grins.

"I applaud your notion of homework," I say, and Jerome just stares at me. His eyes are green and he's got a rash of pale brown birthmarks. "Who are those supposed to be?"

Jerome shrugs.

"I'm a terrible artist," I say. When I'm nervous sometimes I don't stop talking. Alice and Brendan know this about me. Madeline is starting to. "I'm really only good at computers. And baseball. Or at least your mom thinks I'm good at baseball. I think."

"She does," Jerome says. "She's not a liar."

I have heard Lewis tell my mother that, to do anything of note, you need to cheat the system. Jerome draws quick, vicious Xs over two of his pictures, then rips them up.

"If their eyes are crooked, I have to get rid of them," Jerome says. "Otherwise they come to life."

I look out at the grass, which strikes me as extremely green and dead.

"Don't you get tired of everything here looking the same?" I ask.

"It's perfect," Jerome says, and the conversation's over, just like that.

Later, after dinner, I go to the man-made waterfall and throw in torn-up Wonder Bread and the fish attack it, starving. I smoke a whole pack of clove cigarettes, I have no idea why. My chest feels like a chimney. I say it out loud to no one. Then I go to the Mac lab and—with one of the identical rocks—I smash one of the screens.

* * *

The truth is I was sent here for storing drug-free bags of urine in the cabinet under the sink in case one of the older kids needed them in a pinch. I picked the kitchen sink because my mother never looked there. It was Lewis who found them, late at night. I had woken up to pee which I guess is ironic. He rarely slept over. He was wearing the Stanford shirt, holding the bags up by their rubber bands, and he was laughing. "We've got more in common than you think," he said. Before I could respond he put them back under the sink and curled up with my mother on the pull-out couch. The next morning my mother marched into my room, tore off my blanket, and saw the silk moth on my back.

"It's good luck," I said. "It's a symbol of prosperity and reincarnation. Brendan's cousin can do it for you, cheap." It had been weeks since I'd washed my sheets, weeks since my mother went to the dry cleaner. I could feel blackheads itching the sides of my face. I cupped my hands on my cheeks to hide them. Mascara gobbed around my mother's eyes. She never used to wear mascara. I kept waiting for her to yell something.

That night she and Lewis went out. They ate at an expensive French place, little forks and thousand-dollar courses. I knew about the French place because my mother wrote about it; I knew all these things about her, but so did the rest of the world.

A week later the school brochures came. A month later I had my softball mitt and I was on my way.

* * *

Iris says, "I see a lot of potential in you, otherwise I wouldn't bother, you realize that?" and I nod, even though this can't be true. She has to bother, she's a teacher. The campus still looks dry and the sky is red. The classrooms have giant windows so you feel like you are outdoors at all times. In Manhattan you should feel like you live in the air, all those skyscrapers, but instead you feel like you live inside a dirty computer. Why would I want to go back?

I do.

Iris is going on about respect for nature and for property, and I want to say I respect nature, I just don't respect machines. I respect animals but not the way that people cage them. Sometimes I think that in a better world cats would walk with two legs, fish would breathe just fine on dry land, fisherman would really be fucked. Once Madeleine asked if Lewis had a robot like in the movies, a slave made of metal, but even if he'd been given one, he wouldn't use it. He needed people doing his chores to make him feel important.

"It's also your attendance," Iris says. "The brain is a muscle. You don't use it, it goes." She holds her hand out, a fist, lets it fly open, little particles dancing in the air. "Pfft," she says, "it goes just like that."

* * *

I am locked in solitary confinement in the Main house. There are locks but no handcuffs, there is a white comforter and a mattress so soft it is sinking. After I stay silent for 24 hours—I don't even get a visit from Maddie—my mother is called. It is Jerome who tells me, bringing a tray of cut up apples, peanut butter, chamomile tea, wanting to make sure I eat a few bites. Since school started, he has gotten taller, and his hair has gotten blonder, he wears a thin blue sweatshirt with a grinning lion on the front. He stares for a minute, looks around like he's getting his bearings.

"My mom says to tell you your mom's on her way."

Before I can ask for specificity—*How on her way? Thinking about coming? Or actually on the road on her way?* because my mother thinks about a lot of things she doesn't do—Jerome has slipped out of the room, and soon I hear the patter of the tetherball against his hands.

Since Lewis, when I asked my mother about the summer her father predicted the end of the world, she didn't answer. She got very good at coming up with questions that countered questions: "Is the coffee ready?" "What did you think of this article?" "What do you think of this dress?" I'd give up or get wrapped up in zipping up red dresses or being the first pair of eyes in New York to read about the painless removal of blackheads. My mother kissed my forehead and she smelled of flowers. I am not a stubborn person and she is.

Now she is walking across the lawn, and even if I couldn't see her I would hear—the squish of her white boots on the wet grass, Lewis her latest and longest with his hand on the small of her back but she's too fast for him to keep it there. She stops outside by the tetherball court where Jerome and his pudgy friend are drinking juice boxes, gaping at her. Then my mother's in Main; then I'm under the covers pretending to sleep. This place exhausts me, is what I'm going to say, this is draining not stimulating not self-improving and I need to go home, but before my breathing is sleep paced my mother flings open the door.

"Grace, get up."

Time has sped by and it seems my mother hasn't realized it. It's November and she wears a thin lace dress, wine-red lipstick, her dark curls pulled back with a clip. Initially she always seems to be the Disney version of herself. I follow her. I always follow her. I always think, *I did not come out of her, no one could have.* It's especially satisfying to see her standing next to stumpy, plain, tangled Iris.

Iris and my mother pace. My mother might be shivering, but she keeps her wrists stiff, she hides it well. Lewis sits on the porch and chain smokes. I am allowed to sit with him, but as Iris puts it, I am still under house arrest and shouldn't get any bold ideas in my head.

"Your mother has something to tell you," Lewis whispers.

For the first time, my mother seems annoyed by this. She digs her hands—those same white gloves—into his arm.

"I'll tell her in my own time," she tries to whisper, her quiet voice that isn't quiet. "I'll tell her by myself."

I stop myself from saying, "Tell me what?" It's this feeling I sometimes have when my friends make me watch horror movies; I always close my eyes before the inevitable, before the violence starts. Madeline once let me try on her stage blood, lipstick-colored, sticky-sweet like syrup. For once I don't actually want my mother to talk to me. For once I wish Madeleine's adoptive French brother with his big bare tanning-bed tan hands was with me, and it was dark, but it's the middle of the afternoon.

There are certain things it's better not to see or know or understand.

When my mother talks to Iris her expression is so earnest. She keeps nodding. Lewis keeps combing his hair and searching his coat pocket for another cigar. Today he wears a crisp blue button down and sandals; like my mother he has mistaken rural for summer. He is snapping pictures of the dorms and the trees and the lake. He turns to me and says, "This is paradise, you schmuck," then reaches over and gives my hair an awkward little ruffle. I check to see if my mother is watching. The chain of events could go like this: he's pleased, she sees, my mother finally will hug me.

After she has finished talking to Iris and signed a few forms, my mother whispers something to Lewis, who heads to the tetherball court. Then she takes my arm and we start walking. I'm not sure where, but she wants me to lead the way.

We pass Jerome. Lewis is letting him win.

"That's her son," I say. "He's always with her."

When my mother left home she was seventeen and the difference between fifteen and seventeen is that you know what you want to do with your life. My mother, at seventeen, was already editor of the community newspaper, she had already discovered the power of a miniskirt. I came twelve years later, a mistake.

We pass the dorms, we pass the baseball diamond. "She likes you for some reason," my mother says. "They're willing to keep you if you get your act together," and then she repeats the thing Lewis said about paradise. Except my mother doesn't call me a schmuck.

"You know the other thing?" my mother asks, reaching for her cigarette. It's not one of her Menthol Lights, it's electronic. It seems weird here, like a cell phone in an Austen movie.

"Lew really likes it here," my mother says. "Do you know what that means?" When I don't answer she says, "He has extremely high standards. He doesn't usually like anything."

When we reach the river, my mother spreads a blanket I didn't even realize she was carrying. "It's lovely," she says.

"But look," I say, pointing at the waterfall, how obviously fake it is, how she hates fake. I wait for a flash of electricity to materialize, or for her to see the goldfish, trapped together like Alaskan salmon pushing hopelessly upstream. She doesn't. I sit next to her, lean towards her, wanting her to kiss my forehead like she did when I was little and we lived in the first of our apartments, Brooklyn, and we both slept on the pull-out couch. She peels off her white gloves, and I see how old her hands look, her veins thick and bruised and purple. The medicine, Lewis will later explain, her refusal to take blood thinners. Her refusal to try anything un-organic. Her refusal to be a hypocrite.

"Lewis said you had something to tell me," I say, and my mother flicks life into her electronic cigarette, drags from it, and hands it to me.

"Just this once," she says, and I am inhaling the odd mint taste of fake smoke, pretending for her benefit I'm actually enjoying it, and that is when the power goes out.

* * *

This is what Maddie tells me later: at four o'clock the lights in Main turned off and the computer lab switched dark and Iris freaked and sent Jerome and his friend out on bicycles to solve the problem. Outside the change was imperceptible. If we hadn't been in front of the waterfall, if it hadn't flat-out stopped, I wouldn't have noticed.

Water trickles from the lip of the waterfall. I walk closer. Bare, I see that it is metal, nothing but a long, thin shower hose.

"Come see," I say.

"See what?" my mother asks. She lies down, flings her arms over the grass. "Isn't this nice?"

I lie down next to her. Her smell is still real, blooming flowers. She cups her hand right on my shoulder. A reflex, I think, but isn't reflex and instinct kind of the same thing? My mother falls instantly asleep. If the world ended this very minute I think I would be happy. If the world ended this very minute my mother would sleep through it. Like everything, I've forgotten her afternoon naps. I can't leave her like that, and so I pretend to sleep too.

It gets dark early here. Frost comes early too, everything will freeze next month when my mother and Lewis are back with the metal and high-speed everything of New York. As if realizing this my mother shoots up, grabs for her electronic cigarette. I give it to her, and she flicks and flicks frantically, 'til it turns on and she's inhaling nothing and the tip blasts a peak of orange into the dusk that has settled around us. If you look in the direction of the campus you can see the slightest line of end-of-day pink where the sun once was.

"Fucker," my mother says. I've never heard her swear before. Maybe she thinks she's talking to Lewis. "I can't see a damn thing."

"That's because the power's out."

My mother blinks up. "Grace?" Her voice questions even my name. She should have called me something blunter, plainer, dumber. She knows that now.

I think of how my mother wants to look forty when she's sixty. There was a time when this seemed inevitable. Now the inevitable—which neither of us say—is that she will probably never be sixty. My mother has always been beautiful. What else do I tell people about her?

"I know the way back," I say, and I do, but that isn't where we're going. I hold out my hand. I am glad she is wearing her gloves. She is still taller than me. My eyes hover at the soft white ridge of her shoulder. Her fear has a kind of shimmer to it, like a carnival goldfish or a pinned-down butterfly. I follow the man-made waterfall away from campus. I am determined to find a river, a real one, and I am determined to have her with me when

I do this. My mother shivers so hard I can hear the grinding of her jaw. I don't know where I am anymore.

Jerome finds us. Jerome speeds up on a bike I didn't know he had, beaming an enormous flashlight. My mother looks spooked for a moment, then takes his face in her gloves. His flashlight is harsh. I notice new veins in her neck, that same deep purple. On the way back, I ask her to tell us the story about the drought. "I know I'm too old for it," I say, "but Jerome wants to hear."

She actually tells it, my mother. The dehydrated cats drinking spoiled apple juice, the flopping fish, Damien's nightmares, their long walk towards the edge of the world. But the story ends differently this time. This time, out of sheer determination, she and Damien make the water levels rise.

* * *

There's history you can't find, history that changes like cave drawings that morph due to rain and sleet and years. The year Lake Michigan almost dried up there were a few fatalities, or that's what my mother told me when I was seven or maybe eight, but according to Wikipedia and Google, they've been filed away and forgotten. I like to think about the world erasing everything and reinventing itself, a huge scale version of my mother at a spa.

Back at Main House, Lewis whispers, "Did she tell you?" and I don't respond, because my mother's still shaken up about the power, and if the whole world becomes like this, changeable at the flip of a switch, is it a good thing she'll be out of it?

This is a horrible thought to have.

"Make the most of every day, you schmuck," Lewis says, but his voice isn't joking any more.

"I'll try," I say. "I'll try to remember that you're paying for paradise." And Lewis shakes his head, and it seems like we maybe understand each other. He takes my wrist and pulls me close to him.

"I'm getting her the best treatment," he says, and he's the one who hugs me, his coat smelling like an ash tray. "We've got to beat this thing," he says, "we've got to beat the system," and I ask, "Don't you always do that?"

I watch my mother and Lewis step into his car. I've promised to stay and be good, and I am going to be taken out of solitary confinement. My mother calls my name, leans out of the passenger side, kisses the air in the direction of my cheek.

I'm supposed to be at dinner but I can't eat. Rain streams down the windows, leaks onto my bed. There's a knock at my door; I'm expecting Iris, or maybe Maddie with a bagel wrapped in a napkin, or Iris, apologetic, smug, but it's Jerome. He's changed into a button-down shirt and I can see his friend in the hall, hopping from one foot to the other.

"A message from your mom?" I ask, and Jerome looks at his friend, then shakes his head. The friend steps forward, page-like, brown hair cut short around his too-round head. He holds out something wrapped in paper towel. I take it. It's a couple of flowers, purple-blue and totally special, different from all the others.

"There are only a few like this," Jerome says. "You can put them in a vase."

I thank him. I want to ask him if he believes in reincarnation, but he's just a kid, so I take the flowers and pour water into this squat vase my mother gave me for a mint sprig that has long since died.

In two years there will be a chemical spill and the man-made waterfall will be destroyed and the river will be drained and refilled, put on a switch that runs through New England, but I don't know that yet. So I write English papers and I play softball and I study as much as I need to for algebra and sometimes I see Iris leaving for dates, picked up in Pontiacs and beat-up vans, Jerome watching from the porch, her hair brushed and down. I follow Maddie to the soft serve stand, and I hit home runs, and I turn sixteen, and, when I try, very hard, I barely think about my mother at all.

JENNY HAYDEN HALPER'S *stories have appeared in* Our Stories *(Emerging Writer Award Winner),* Southeast Review *(Pushcart Prize nominee),* Joyland, PANK, *the*

Chicago Tribune Printer's Row, *and elsewhere, and her story collection has been a finalist for the St. Lawrence Book Prize and the Hudson Prize. She also works as a screenwriter and heads development for Maven Screen Media.*

Beyond Reproach
Kristin Burcham

It only happened because of the wink. We were in an early morning faculty meeting in the middle school library. Our administrators hammered through the agenda items with pleading eyes. Too many teachers scheduling tests on the same day. Attendance records not being kept correctly. Don't overuse the copy machine—too expensive. And don't assign too much homework. Parents asking why their children's backpacks were so heavy. Parents asking why we didn't assign more books. Each complaint battered us until we all looked beaten down. The first bell had yet to ring and already I longed for a nap.

Mrs. Blenheim raised her hand. She was a veteran teacher, a woman like me, roughly my age, but newly transferred to our school, a star player brought in to erase poor Wendell who had left in disgrace. Newbies on our staff—no matter who—would be wise to stay quiet at meetings until they've been in the trenches with us for at least a year, but Mrs. Blenheim's arm was high, bold and unapologetic.

"I've created a new rubric for each of my assignments to better assess how close students are to the learning targets and mastering the standards, thus guiding differentiated instruction for reteaching and equitable access to the content," Mrs. Blenheim said, spouting the jargon of the moment with ease. We all stared at her.

A pause; then the entire room surged. Teachers were muttering and indignant, tilting eyebrows, jutting chins. The principal and his assistant looked dazzled. Mrs. Blenheim was stoic. She straightened her already straight spine, caught my eye, and winked.

It was as if a tunnel of light had beamed between us. I flushed suddenly, deeply, feeling both flattered and confused. Had she been kidding? Maybe she knew how ridiculous she sounded and enjoyed riling up the troops. Or was she telling me that I was like her: devoted, exceptional, an inspired teacher? Then she must not have realized that I had been on autopilot for years. Or was it something else?

"I'd like to see your rubrics," I said.

She was wiry, like a boy. I envied her upper arms, freely displayed in the strappy clothes she wore, while I spent hours in stores trying to find a dress or a shirt with concealing sleeves. We were cordial colleagues. Mornings, we greeted each other in the office when we signed in. During assemblies, we worked together to monitor kids too overstimulated to stay quiet or sit still. We taught the same subject, middle school English, but she was credentialed to teach in multiple subject areas. She did not let me forget this. We were not close.

But then, she winked at me. And I was aflame.

When the meeting was over, she marched down the hall to her classroom, preening. Are you ready for Open House? Mrs. Blenheim is. Do you know the first names of your students' parents? Mrs. Blenheim does. Have you posted lesson plans for the entire year on the school website? Mrs. Blenheim has. She slipped into her room and closed the door, graceful and emphatic. We both worked hard but she exuded a thrill, like an explorer on the brink of a world-shaking discovery, while I plowed on, assiduous and highly effective, yes, but a lumbering ox.

When school ended that day, I went into her classroom. She glanced up at me from her desk chair, pen poised, waiting. I was supposed to ask about the rubrics. Or she was supposed to offer.

complaints? That's good. Tell me more." My husband shifted in his chair of animal skin.

As we drove home, I gazed at women on the sidewalks, coming out of stores or going into office buildings. I looked at them and then checked my insides, to see if I wanted them, their lips or curves or skin, but I didn't feel any tingling, any hidden desire. I studied those who walked alone, gliding down the street without a man holding their hand, no one pinioning them down. Did I want to be one of them? I saw older women, their bodies asymmetrical, holding a heavy handbag or navigating uncomfortable heels. Was that me? I rested my forehead against the window, feeling suffocated as Cliff steered us home. The women on the sidewalks shrank from view, but I could hear their footsteps thrumming in my ears.

I got home and acted as if nothing had changed. Cliff did the same. He sat at the kitchen table, scrolling through his phone, waiting for me to serve him lunch. I scooted around the kitchen, made sandwiches. I thought if I acted normally, I would begin to feel that way. But then my phone rang. It was Nathan Kitrell, the school principal. Such a call wasn't unheard of, but it was rare.

"It's Nathan," I blurted.

Cliff stopped eating. "Pick up!"

"Hello?" I tried to keep my voice natural. Nathan could be calling about anything, not necessarily Mrs. Blenheim. Why did I hope that he was?

Nathan spoke but Cliff was mouthing at me: *What is it? What does he want?* and something else, so I turned to the wall, trying to focus.

"I'm sorry, could you say that again?"

Nathan cleared his throat. "An allegation has been made," he said.

"Of what?" I squeezed my eyes shut.

"A possible test security incident."

Was there a less sexy phrase in the English language?

"Come see me first thing in the morning," he said.

I put my phone down and turned to Cliff.

He frowned at me. "Well?"

"I don't know. It's not about that. Something about the state tests."

Cliff sighed, relieved, I suppose, but I thought, now, now he will say something, demand answers, smear his thumb across my straying lips. Instead, he pushed his plate away, picked up his own phone and peered at it over his glasses. He grunted at something he saw there, then stood and walked away as if he weren't carrying the screen but following it, trotting into his study as obediently as a dog on a leash.

I cleared the table and scrubbed away the remains of our lunch before loading the dishwasher. It was silly, but if I didn't, the food crusted on the plates.

* * *

No one wants to be called into the principal's office, not even an adult, but the next morning I appeared as requested. A poster on his wall exhorted, *Integrity is doing the right thing when no one else is looking*. I did not want to do Mr. Kitrell's right thing. I was tired of it. I wanted to stay in my chair when the Pledge of Allegiance came on the loudspeaker. I wanted to tell an overbearing parent the truth about her *gifted* child. I wanted someone to be listening, someone to be looking.

Nathan wore a bow tie. He looked scrubbed and wholesome, as if he were an aging soda jerk from small-town Iowa.

"You've been at this school for a long time," he said.

"Yes," I said, "even longer than you." I crossed my arms and thought of the sharp scent of Mrs. Blenheim's shampoo. "I'm turning fifty in a few months."

"Your students' most recent test scores? They were very good."

"I haven't decided yet how to celebrate my birthday," I said. Suddenly this felt very important.

"Your students' scores are, perhaps, too good."

"How did you celebrate your fiftieth?" I said, leaning forward, truly wanting to know, to get some ideas.

"I did a weekend in Palm Springs."

He looked down at a file on his desk. My heartbeat scuttled in my chest.

Instead, neither of us spoke. I just stood there, looking at her, knowing that I had come for something and that I didn't want to leave. At last I moved to stand behind her at her desk and placed my hands on the tops of her shoulders. Her muscles were hard, taut beneath her skin's surface, but that skin was soft and warm, as if she had just stepped from a hot shower. My gut shifted in a commotion I had not felt for ages, while Mrs. Blenheim stayed motionless, with no change in breath or sound. Like a Buddha. My excitement swelled.

I wasn't sure what to do next; I leaned over and kissed the top of her head. Her hair was pulled back tight, in a bun. Her scalp was pale and smelled of astringent shampoo. I couldn't see her expression. My kiss felt right, if daring. It felt like the truest thing I had done in a long time.

* * *

I've always secretly admired mimes, how a white-gloved hand slaps against the air and an invisible wall appears—once I stepped a toe outside, I could suddenly see the box trapping me. I had been married to a good man for many years, been an upstanding teacher for even longer, but—*Look*!—I could still be unpredictable, even if I was approaching fifty. I now remembered the thrill of surprising myself. Had security cameras once captured me, in the heady days before Cliff proposed, lifting my dress for him in the hotel garden? He had quivered in disbelief as I unzipped his pants, astonished as I lowered myself onto his lap. I knew it was a favorite memory and had served to arouse him countless times in the following years, but it was so long ago, it was as if those were two different people. Strangers. I could never do something like that now, would never think to, but it hardly mattered—Cliff would never let me.

That night, as we lay reading in bed before lights out, I watched him from the corners of my eyes. When 10:30 arrived, Cliff closed his book, reached over, and turned out his bedside lamp, but I kept mine on. I told him about Mrs. Blenheim. He's a pale man. He grew paler.

"You did what?" he said.

"I kissed her hair."

He turned his light back on.

"Did she respond?"

"No."

"Did you do anything else?"

"No."

"You could be charged with sexual harassment."

I rolled my eyes. He didn't see because he was grabbing his phone.

"It's late but I can leave a message for Larry," he said. "We'll see what the legal ramifications are."

From kiss to lawsuit: all-or-nothing thinking, my husband's specialty. I've read that it's a common cognitive distortion, but self-help books don't do much if the wrong person is reading them and Cliff disdained "pop psychology claptrap." There was nothing I could do to keep him from accelerating from zero to sixty, and if I tried, he would look at me, not angry, but hurt, as if I hadn't been paying attention. I waited for him to ask why I had kissed Mrs. Blenheim, but he didn't, so I stayed quiet as he dialed our lawyer. I waited for him to become a jealous husband, but no, nothing, so I didn't protest when he asked for an appointment for the following day. I didn't even point out that I would need to use one of my paid sick days, the ones he wanted me to save. He spent his days as an internal auditor at Wickham/Barnett. Let him do the math.

* * *

We went to Larry's office, an overstuffed room that looked as if it had been lifted out of a movie set. Thick mahogany shelves lined with books. Capacious leather chairs in oxblood red. A brass banker's lamp with a green glass shade. No one raised their voices. Larry tipped his graying head toward me and asked questions, not the same ones I had hoped for from Cliff, but at least he asked. I looked at the wall of books and described the faculty meeting in the library as Larry scribbled notes on a yellow legal pad. His voice sounded calm, inviting. "So she winked at you without provocation? No one saw you kiss her? She hasn't lodged any

"Was Palm Springs fun?" I said. Palm Springs is a gay mecca, I thought. Dinah Shore Invitational. Maybe he was trying to give me a hint. "My husband doesn't like the desert. He's prone to skin cancers."

"Really."

"He has something removed almost every year. Usually around the nose. They have never been a big deal, but they always scare me. I try to keep him out of the sun."

Nathan's look was hard to read. Disbelief? Or maybe pity.

"Are you careful to apply sunscreen?" I said. The manila folder gleamed between us, as if it were winking at me too.

"We need to talk about your students' test results," he said.

* * *

My jangly excitement was now a sharp drop in my bowels. Why did it feel good? I should want to recapture my boredom. I should want to feel safe again. I strode down the hall. Mrs. Blenheim. What had she done? What would she say to me? I went upstairs to the second floor and approached the light shining through the small rectangular window set into her classroom door, but when I tried the knob, it was locked. The room was empty.

* * *

That evening when Cliff got home from work, I told him, "Nathan said my students' test scores were outstanding this year."

I didn't tell him about the accusation of cheating then; that wasn't what I wanted to talk about. He still had not expressed any jealousy over my kissing Mrs. Blenheim, only concern about my job or a lawsuit. There was a shimmering disapproval, as if he were my parent and not my husband. Cliff wanted to protect our routines. He wanted to take turns watering the lawn, eat salmon on Thursday nights, pay the bills before the first of the month. He wanted the peace and tranquility of retirement, only he wanted them before we had retired.

"Good for you," he said. "Keep it up."

After dinner, I sank into my nightly bath, the hot sudsy water embracing me. My fingers snaked their way between my legs, deft, knowing. Cliff watched TV in the room below, unconcerned; more wrongdoing on my part would be inconceivable to him. I strummed, insistently, my water-softened skin reminded me of Mrs. Blenheim's shoulders. Was it her finger pointing at me, singling me out, implicating that I had helped my students with the state test? The possibility made me shiver.

I did not tell Cliff until later that night, when the lights were off and we lay beside each other in bed.

"There was another reason Nathan called me in," I said. "I stand accused."

"Accused? Oh God."

Ask, I thought. Ask about the kiss. Ask why I did it—maybe then *I* could figure it out. Ask what it felt like. Cliff's lips were faintly visible in the darkened room. They should not have touched anyone else's lips but mine in the last seventeen years, but now I wished they had. I wished that he had felt the sudden urge to kiss someone and that he had done it and that it had churned his insides to oatmeal.

"It's not that," I said. "My students' test scores are so good, I'm accused of cheating."

"Are you kidding?" he said. "I'll call Larry in the morning."

* * *

The morning bell had already rung before I reached my classroom the next day. The students looked at me suspiciously, as if I were up to something. Would there be a pop quiz? They all wanted the usual class procedure. They wanted to start with the warm-up on the board. They would groan as if they hated it, resented the relentless exercises that began the day, but secretly they needed them, loved the safety of knowing what to do, following the routine. It would tell them that the world was spinning on its axis, that life was fair, that the bright future they deserved was guaranteed. But no, here was their teacher, tardy, dawdling.

I leaned on the edge of my desk and surveyed the students. Their eyes were glazed with sleep and distrust. Bernardo raised his hand.

"What are we doing today?" he said. A question that would normally irritate me. The agenda was always written on the board. Only it wasn't.

"What do you think we should do?" I asked.

Rumbles. Rattled laughter. "Sleep," called out one boy. "Nothing!" shouted a girl. Others looked around. This was anarchy. Talking without first raising your hand. Asking for what you thought you wanted.

"I've had some news," I said.

"Uh oh," Bernardo said.

"Your test scores were excellent. Even better than last year's class. I think I've taught you everything you need to know right now."

"Right," someone said.

"She's up to something," muttered the girl who wore purple every day.

"Is this reverse psychology?" asked the star student.

"She's out to trick us," said purple girl.

I clasped my hands as if in prayer, trying to show my sincerity. A few of the kids copied me, thinking that was what I wanted.

"I want us to try something different," I said, standing tall. "Something new. Who can tell me what the word *spontaneous* means?"

Several hands shot up. At last, something familiar, being asked to define a word. But I didn't call on them.

"Let's be spontaneous!" I said. "Who can come up here and do something spontaneous?"

The kids looked at each other.

"Who wants to sing?" I asked. "Dance? Maybe you have a funny joke to tell!"

Silence.

"Take out a piece of paper," said Bernardo.

"Write your name, period, and date in the upper right-hand corner," said the star student.

Binders were being opened, pencil pouches unzipped.

"No, I meant it," I said.

A boy in the front row got up and wrote the correct date on the whiteboard. The girl never ready with her required materials had paper in front of her, a pencil in hand.

"What's the title of the assignment?" said Bernardo.

I looked at the classroom door. No eyes peered through the little window. I looked at the students, staring at me expectantly. Purple girl was rocking in her seat, agitated.

"Semester Vocabulary Review," I said. "We'll prepare early for the final. Don't forget to capitalize your title."

Heads bent over desks and a quiet scribbling descended on us all.

* * *

I went into the faculty women's room. Mrs. Blenheim stood at the sink, washing her hands. She was humming and did not stop when I came in. The door closed behind me.

"You said something to the principal," I said.

"I did," she said.

She crossed over to me. I wasn't sure what this meant. If it was good or bad.

"May I?" she asked. She gestured to the paper towel dispenser. I was blocking her way.

"I didn't mean to offend you."

Her hands were dripping on the floor.

"No offense taken. But we must be beyond reproach."

"We?"

"The school. If one teacher's scores are compromised, our whole school is vulnerable. Our district."

"I just wanted to be close. To someone." Only as I said it did I realize it was true.

She reached around me, pulled the brown paper towel and then wiped her hands fastidiously, drying between her fingers, dabbing her wrists.

"What's happening?" I asked. "Are you angry?"

"No," she said.

"Did you want to be close to me?" My breath caught in my chest.

She folded the damp towel into a neat square.

"My students' scores are impeccable," she said. She smiled, sadly. "Dear. I expect to receive the Golden Apple Award."

She leaned forward and placed her cheek against mine. It was lotion-soft, and I thought I could feel the brush of miniscule hairs, a feathery down that could have been from either or both of us. Her lips were close to my ear.

"I admire you," she said. "You poor thing."

My lungs shriveled.

Using her square of paper towel, she opened the bathroom door to leave, her clean hand protected from contact with germs.

* * *

I didn't go back to class. The fob I lugged around had all my keys—car, school, home—so I just dashed out of the bathroom, down the hall, out the side stairs and to the faculty parking lot. No one was there. Sensible cars, clean and economical, were lined up in their assigned spaces. I climbed into my Honda and turned on the ignition wishing it would roar to life, that I could peel out, loud and fiery, but the engine turned reasonably over. I yanked the steering wheel at the exit, but the tires didn't screech. I accelerated down the street faster than I had ever done, far above the school zone limit, but there was no one else on the road, no cop waiting to punish me.

I flew past a stop sign hearing a horn bleat as I turned left instead of my usual right. Now there were a few cars around, although they seemed to be making space for me, slowing down, changing lanes, giving the crazy driver plenty of room. I gripped the wheel and accelerated, pushing through one yellow light and then another, with no clear idea of where I was headed until I saw taller buildings in the distance, the glass and steel clusters of downtown. Cliff. I needed to see him. Now.

As the streets grew more congested, I was forced to slow down, past the new open-air food mart, past the old post office being converted into condos, past the parking lots and the rundown stores, into the sleek corridor of the financial section where trees and fountains and strangely bright green grass sprouted from cement planters. I parked across from the Wickham/Barnett tower, a metered space that only allowed for fifteen minutes, the kind of spot that we usually laughed at: Who would pay so much for so little? I walked away without feeding the meter.

I didn't know what I was going to say. I tugged at one of the heavy glass doors and crossed the gleaming lobby, trying to think, but the words in my brain were spidery and uneven, like the black-veined marble surrounding the elevator. The ride lurched upward past a dozen floors, and the doors pinged open. In the reception area, Sandy wasn't at her curved desk. A young man I had never seen before came out of the nearest office, but I brushed right by him, straight, then a right, and then there was Cliff's office, the door open, he and Sandy bent over some papers he held. They both looked up at me.

Sandy smiled. "Mrs.—"

"Get out," I said.

Sandy's smile vanished. Cliff looked surprised, then displeased.

"Get out," I repeated. "I need to talk to my husband."

Cliff and Sandy exchanged glances. "Honey, I don't know what this is about, but…"

Sandy stepped around me and out the door. It was still wide open.

Cliff neatly placed his papers on his desk. I opened my mouth to speak but nothing came out. A familiar ripple below his razor-edged sideburns told me that he was clenching his jaw. Sobs began to rise in my chest.

"I miss you," I whispered. "I miss you so much."

He came toward me. "I'm here," he said, and cupped my face in his hands, using the edges of his thumbs to smooth my tears away. "I'm right here."

I shook my head.

"Not you."

His face stiffened and he dropped his arms.

"I miss *you*," I said. "The old you. The real you, the one I remember." I swallowed hard. "I miss old *me* too."

He sighed and put his hands on my shoulders. He said, gently, "The truth is," and he moved his face close to mine, "what you need to know is"—he came closer still—"I never really liked either of them all that much."

Then he pulled me forward and wrapped his arms around me, pressing me into him, his shirt buttons against my wet face, the top of my head tucked beneath his chin. He held me tightly and I reached up behind him, the pads of my fingers slipping against the smooth surface of his dry-cleaned shirt, trying to find purchase, wanting to cling, to his back, to his shoulder blades, to this person I had married, and I heard a click as someone—I don't know who—quietly shut the door.

KRISTIN BURCHAM'S *work has appeared in* The Journal of Compressed Creative Arts, Dogwood: A Journal of Poetry and Prose, The Writer's Chronicle, *and most recently in the award-winning* Healing Visions: An Anthology of Micro Prose and Fine Art Photography. *She received her MFA in Creative Writing from Vermont College of Fine Arts and lives in Santa Monica, California.*

Sow

Allison Backous Troy

My mother texts me a list of her seed collection: *milkweed, sunflowers, bachelor buttons, daisies, zinnias, hollyhocks.* She has spent the summer collecting them on her daily walks to the grocery store, her neighbor's plants pushing through the wire fences lining her East Chicago neighborhood. A few blocks away, the local BP petroleum plant's burning flare towers blow fumes just above her street before they push out over Lake Michigan, its rocky beach dotted with mini plastic liquor bottles.

It is ugly where my mother lives, and gray, but she stops to collect seeds where she sees them, her list shared with me each time she adds a new plant to her litany of what she can grow. It's something she's always done. I remember her pinching a single baby spider plant from a display at the mall and putting it in her pocket. That spider plant is still living, twenty-five years later, its striped leaves dangling brightly down the side of her bookcase.

And I am jealous of that plant, jealous of the seeds my mother has stowed away so eagerly, her nurturing tendencies aimed at flowers and not her own children, not at me.

My mother is abusive, has abused me. It's a fact, an immovable one: she has not only done me harm, but she is unable to stop doing harm. *Unable* is what I have to say because, if I linger on the other fact, that she has often *chosen* to harm me, I freeze. I grew up listening to her own stories of fear—her absent mother, her alcoholic father, the fists and the black eyes and the rage—and I watched her pick up her place in that cycle, her own rages spilling over me. I have had to sow my own life very deliberately in response to all this, and while I have dug deeply into my friendships, my marriage, and my own motherhood, I still freeze, the fear she planted years ago stretching its long roots too deep in me to rip out.

What makes my mother such a master grower? How is it that her little backyard is a tiny prairie full of wildflowers, that her tomato plants are always bent over with the red fruit we both love? As a child, I remember my mother cutting up ripe tomatoes for me and setting them in a wooden bowl, sprinkling them with salt. We ate them together on the kitchen floor and we were happy. When I eat tomatoes now, I cut them and salt them and think of telling her that I'm eating one of our favorite snacks. I think of telling her that I love her. I finish my tomatoes and drink their juices from the bowl, seeds and salt together.

Part of this tension between what she can grow and what she can love is that my mother is just a natural gardener. She has the knack, the green thumb; she knows what needs watering and what needs left alone. While my father escaped their unhappy marriage via martinis and classic movies, my mother chose dirt, geraniums, the petunias that she remembered trumpeting over the edge of her father's porch. When she came home from work, she often stood in the backyard garden before entering the house, silent and still among her hand-grown cosmos. And if I came out to say hi or to ask about dinner, I got nothing, her mouth tight and angry that someone had walked into her small patch of Eden, uninvited.

That's the hard part for me, that I often felt so outside the sphere of what my mother loved. I knew as a child that whatever love she had for my father was dying and that she didn't want to tend it any longer. She was letting it rot, become soil for her own escape. And there were reasons to escape: our poverty, our tiny house, my father's own disdain for the woman he had married, the nights she spent popping Heinekens and weeping over what her own childhood had and hadn't been. She remembered very little about her own mother.

"I don't know how to be a mom, because of her," she would cry, the yellow kitchen light spilling over the table. As a girl, I hid in my room while she cried, but when I got older, I put away childish things and took a seat at the table, learning how to be quiet, listening to her cry. "You're the only one who understands," she would say, and my whole heart swelled up, so glad that I was finally someone she could, or would, love.

But what was sown between us there was not love, or at least, good love. I learned that to be loved by my mother meant to be everything to her but a daughter: therapist, grocery shopper, chauffeur, wailing wall, dumpster. After my father left, my mother moved us into a trailer with her new boyfriend. "This is my time," she told me, and I nodded eagerly, wanting to see her happy. Her boyfriend would later kick her in the face with a steel-toed boot. It was one of many things he did, and what I did, in those days, was pretend to be a mother, or at least, my mother's mother, the one she never had, my own voice clear and calm as I made 911 calls, as I put a wet washcloth on my mother's swollen eye. "You are going to be okay, Mom," I said, her whole body heaving. "It is going to be okay. I am here."

What else could I do? I wanted my mother's love. She wanted something else. And I mothered her in those moments, and so many others, and what grew from our reversed bond was sad and hungry and mean and lonely. Money would go missing from my wallet; she would ask me to give her a ride to Walgreens and then walk to the bar across the street. "You don't have to pick me up," she would say, stepping out of the car in shoes that came out of my closet. I bought groceries and paid electric bills, forging her signature to keep our lights on. And when I did go to college, I would call home and could hear my mother suck her teeth: "Well, what's up?" she would say, and I could feel how tight-lipped she was, how angry. If I wasn't tending her, I was a weed, something she could pluck if she wanted. If she felt like it.

But my mother felt like caring for her garden and houseplants. She gave them time, and water, and care. Her pots were always blooming with plants she rescued from the grocery store; seed packets were stacked on her nightstand. When she left that trailer, she brought the spider plant, but her new house didn't have a bed for me. Her plants seemed easier for her—easier to care for, to enjoy, to want. What made it so easy to love plants more than your own child? What did gathering seeds do for my mother that my own love could not?

When my son was born, I hoped that my mother would be excited. Instead, she was afraid of holding him, almost dropping his tiny body on the floor. She flipped between terror and belligerence, completely overcome by nerves and also enraged that I was now a "real" mother, protective of my own child. When she told me that she and my son had "gone potty together," I felt my shoulders arch, like wings. "You don't go potty with your grandson, Mom. You don't pull down your pants in front of him. You won't do that again." She tried, again, during my son's bath, and when I told her to leave, she marched outside and urinated behind my apartment. She came back with that tight-lipped smile, rank with piss, delighted with my shock. "It was my time to go," she said. "My time."

She's never come to my home again. Nor will she. What other answer is there? She's apologized, but what is there to do but leave her alone, for my son's sake, for mine? She texts me updates on her health: carotid stenosis, arthritis, increases in anxiety meds. She lets me know that she's gotten a diagnosis—borderline personality disorder—and that she is trying to hold herself together. I turn to Google and learn that borderline, when not caught, creeps into the heart like bindweed, the invasive vine that my neighbors salt and burn in their yards. Bindweed's roots can crack stone, and its flowers are like the white petunias my mother keeps on her porch: simple, pretty, insidious. It has taken my mother over sixty years to get a diagnosis, and salt and fire might not be enough to keep our hearts from cracking.

What do you do when you've lived your life without your parent, even though they were right there? What could grow green between us, my mother and I? What could possibly take root, and stay?

Milkweed, maybe; zinnias, sunflowers, pansies. I go to the garden center and pick up what feels familiar. In the plague years of Covid, I finally have a garden that's growing. I have tried cultivating my own flower preferences—I look for plants native to my home in western Colorado, for mallow and columbine, for blooms that I can call my own. But I always circle back to my mother's seed litany, those easy, common flowers that seem to grow anywhere, my own zinnias bobbing their fuchsia heads long into October.

And, afraid as I am, as I will always be, I text her what I'm growing: *petunias, sunflowers, cosmos, white lavender, poppies, red yarrow, Indian paintbrush.* I send her photos of my red sunflowers, their velvet heads rising high above my deck, and of the pansies that stayed alive all winter, their blue and yellow faces resting on snow. She texts me back—*your flowers truly make me smile.* Days later, I get an envelope in the mail full of seeds, seeds from my mother's garden. Seeds she's gathered for me.

I do not know how old the seeds are, if they'll grow, or if they really have a place in my garden. Should I sow what my mother has given me? Are seeds stronger than mental illness, or emotional scars, or fear? I think of what my mother might have done, if her mother had sent her seeds. If she had stayed. I think of what might have been. I think of what I can do, myself, my son's face beaming over the kitchen table, cherry tomatoes in his bowl. I know what I can grow. And I make room for those seeds in my garden, the milkweed stratifying in cold winter dirt, my mother's garden planted, with mine.

ALLISON BACKOUS TROY *is a writer living in the valley of Grand Junction, Colorado. She's a midwestern transplant to* *the west and is currently working on a "natural history" of her childhood in Chicago's postindustrial south suburbs. She holds an MFA from Seattle Pacific University, and has been published in* Image, St. Katherine's Review, *and* Crab Orchard Review.

The Wedding Dress
Dyanne Stempel

The night before my wedding, I'm wearing high-waisted palazzo pants, snug around my ass, with a shimmery, gold halter that offers a stunning panorama of my boobs. For the last month, I've been on a cabbage soup regime—"the bridal diet!" my mother called it when she sent the link. I look hot.

My wedding dress, a puff pastry of organza and silk, stews behind my bedroom door. The dress and I have been at war since the beginning. I have tried to make peace with it, invite it into my life. It is, after all, a dress that when modeled so exceptionally in the catalogue, promised domestic bliss, generations of it, starting with me. But silently, behind its satin tail, its Hasidic neckline, the vises it calls sleeves, I mock it. It makes me feel unworthy, trying to noose hundreds of tiny button necks into their hole mates.

It's a restless night for Los Angeles in June, the heat like a persistent firing squad of blow dryers. Baby Santa Anas, wicked and erratic even in their infancy, capsize the floating candles my mother has earlier coaxed into the pool—little yachts, they dance one moment, suicide the next. I crouch by the side of the pool to right the candles, relight them, but it's no use. Metaphor, Rachel would call that if she were here, although I am beginning to doubt she'll show.

still time to run, she texted yesterday.

Across the pool, amidst the party guests, my soon-to-be husband laughs with my sister and her husband and I'm genuinely happy he fits in so well. Less work for me. Not like the last boyfriend, a man so exuberant and luminous, so feral. I miss him, the last one, miss going dark for days with him in his rank studio, getting high and fucking. I am trading up, or at least trading in, because living in the spectacular is no way to live.

I hear Rachel inside, finally, her low, raspy voice, and something deep inside me leaps. As I walk through the sliding glass doors into the living room, my father reaches for me. "Guess who the cat dragged in?" he says, doing something odd and jazzy with his right hand which makes him look like he's unveiling Rachel, like he's a prize model on *The Price is Right*. We all laugh even though it's so lame. Mine is an awful falsetto laugh to quell the awkwardness. Rachel and I haven't seen each other in two years, not since our joint thirtieth birthday party, and no matter what has or hasn't transpired between us we still fumble into each other, stand entwined as the party spins around, as my father, fidgety on the outskirts of our embrace, finally walks away. Neither of us has any inkling, it seems, to let go first. Like a portal back to an ancient time of secrets and forts and diaries with locks, a whole life together in stories, it's all here in this embrace.

Rachel smells, as always, like gardenias and the musky, chai-like hair oil she uses to tame her blond frizz. For forever she has wanted my long, straight cinnamon hair and I've always enjoyed this, her wanting bits of me.

"You look good," she whispers in my hair.

"I know," I say. I've cleaned up my act since last we saw each other which is why she sounds surprised. My puffy face, bloodshot eyes, the apathy and exhaustion, they are things of the past. Even the dirt has been raked from under my fingernails. If there's a hint of bitterness in her tone—that someone, not her, could right the ship this time—I choose to ignore it.

"Come," I say and put my hand on the small of Rachel's back to guide her outside. My parents' house, a low-slung, stucco U, wraps around the pool; sliding glass doors in nearly every main room empty into the garden. We head to the chaise lounges at one end of the pool, far from the other guests to an unlit space near railings where the view of the city, twinkly like a million open Tiffany boxes, is expansive and pretty only at night. By day it's a palette of muck—tall, blocky office towers hidden behind a thick, cottony smudge of brown eyeshadow. We grew up in this city, more noxious each time I visit. Manhattan, where I now live, is a valley of light and shadow chopped into tall, thin boxes. It makes so much more sense. Rachel chose to stay here for college, for law school, for her job at a big downtown law firm. But I wanted to get as far from home as I could, leaving for good when I went east for college. I never considered moving back.

"No one will bother us here," I say, though no one has bothered me all night, not really. All of them, my parents' friends, seem skittish around me. It's my parents who are being feted, who have successfully married me off against all odds. Engaging me in extended conversation of any kind may break the spell.

Rachel and I grab two flutes of pink champagne from a waiter's tray even though I hate champagne, the cloying fizz. It makes me logy and headachy when I just want to be buzzed.

"Where's the mister?" Rachel asks. I point across the pool and watch Rachel's eyes settle onto him, then deaden. I see what she does, an unexceptional man nearing forty, softening midsection, a herniated disc. Ambling through a museum or a ShopRite, not leisurely, but prudently, without arrogance. I find it very comforting.

"You should give him a chance, you know. He's actually very funny and sweet."

"He's awkward," Rachel says.

"*Love* him," I command.

* * *

Rachel hasn't seen the mister since our thirtieth birthday party either, a party we threw for ourselves at Rachel's place in LA. I'd flown in from New York for the weekend and by pure happenstance, a work friend of Rachel's had brought him along. At some point during the party, soon after he introduced himself to me, Rachel asked him to make a margarita, but he didn't know how.

"Seriously?" she said to him. That was strike one. Strike two was when, nine weeks after we met, he quit his full professorship in Los Angeles to move to New York to work on his second book and find a new teaching job. "So clingy and so fast," Rachel said. "He's cornering you."

"Maybe I want to be cornered," I said. I was walking to the subway, on my way to work, and she and I were face timing, as we did daily. "He knows what he wants. I respect that," I said to her five by two pixelated face.

"He's unworthy of you, Tessie," she said.

"I'm unhinged. With no self-respect. How unworthy could he be?" I gave her a wide, ugly smile before stepping down into the subway and hanging up. Strike three.

Rachel stopped speaking to me then. *Choose*, she was saying. She did this periodically. Served me with divorce papers whenever I strayed from our sisterhood, made choices she determined contrary to my real needs or desires. And she was, even if I never told her so, mostly right about those choices. She was like the mirror I instinctively, greedily grabbed to scan myself, all my illogic, my selfishness, and dark longings, before hurriedly covering. No one wants to know the truth about themselves, not really. Besides, I love Rachel, will always love her the way I did when we were eight and nine and ten. A few weeks, a month, however long it took, I waited her out. You only get so many first friends. When she eventually came back, which she always did, it was as if a part of me came back too. An early, softer part of me that, with time, like an unlined face, I could no longer locate on my own.

* * *

"Feng Shui her," the mister said to me one night in bed soon after he'd proposed. I'd been periodically staring, thumb poised, at Rachel's number on my phone, because there was no one I wanted to tell more but also less about my engagement.

"Make room for something better," he said. He was referring to himself, of course. I chalked up his reference to the Chinese arts as a product of the year he spent teaching English in Beijing. He owns a book called *Clearing your Clutter with Feng Shui* which you wouldn't expect him to feature so prominently in his library otherwise cluttered with biographies of Hitler and Stalin. Something about his obsession with fascist strongmen appealed to me. Not just his quest for knowledge but his desire to seek out evidence of how easily social order can devolve. He's not good with chaos which made me realize he was in love with a person I was not, but with his help would become. And this, I finally understood, was the strong appeal of marriage: the relief, the allure of no longer being forced to be myself out there in the open terrain of the world. My other half—a term I had once found so detestable, as if I could only begin to be with someone else—could now do the work.

He took the phone out of my hand that night, lifted my t-shirt up around my neck and palmed my boob. My instinct was to shove him away. That feeling I get when the space around me, already so limited, is sucked up. I refrained as he made his way down the duvet, kissing my ribs, my belly button, the putty webbing of stretchmarks inside my thighs—sinewy leftovers of my fat thin, fat thin yo-yo-ing. He was generous like that, going down on me for a goddamn eternity. My body was slow to respond knowing there was no impediment to our relationship, nothing forbidden. It put a boot on my desire.

* * *

"Please tell me he didn't get down on one knee in Hawaii or some other shithole," Rachel says as we watch blue flame lick the black fake rock of the firepit on this side of the pool.

"Hawaii is *such* a shithole," I say. "It's like the Disneyland of shitholes."

"Let's never go there."

"In Riverside Park," I say. "He proposed there."

He'd actually proposed at a Mattress City in Brooklyn as we tried to bounce on memory foam. He was shopping for his new bed, for his new apartment. Why not make it a marital bed? Make it our apartment. But Rachel would have called that manipulative. I called it practical, lovingly so. And the symbolism, its conjugality, although on the nose, was quite poetic.

"Then he called my dad to ask permission." I blurt this out because I could keep only so much to myself.

"Christ," she says. "Did the medieval king trade your hand for a military alliance with Switzerland?"

"Germany," I say. "The Swiss are too warmongering."

"You. Funny," she says in a way that makes funny sound depressing.

Music floats up from somewhere down the hill. I stand a bit unsteadily to look out over the railing, to the house below us. Lit tiki torches around yet another pool. What were they celebrating down there? A graduation? An engagement? Retirement? One night I'll crisscross these hills, hills beaten into submission by colonies of swimming pools and faux-Tuscan terracotta, to celebrate all the interchangeable milestones across time.

In my periphery I see the mister walk towards us. Rachel sees him too because she stands and joins me at the railing, her shoulder sliding behind mine. He's about to say hello to her, maybe even lean in to awkwardly hug her, but she turns suddenly, without acknowledging him, excuses herself and walks inside. Before he can say anything, I kiss him—his stubble-less cheek with its lime and cedar aftershave—a little offering, because we both know that I will follow her. He moves his chin in Rachel's direction.

"Go," he says, not unkindly but not warmly either.

* * *

Rachel is in my bedroom, sitting on my childhood bed. I cross the room to sit next to her. We both stare at the back of the door and the dress stares back. I have backup now and the dress knows it.

"Why is it a thing that you're not supposed to let the groom see you in the dress before the wedding?" I ask.

"You mean your last moment of spectacle and power before all your rights cease to exist?" Rachel says. "It's probably when marriages were arranged, and the man could cancel before the wedding if he thought you looked like a duck ass ho."

"I'm actually a big fan of arranged marriage," I say. "You get to blame someone else when things go south. We should insist all marriage be arranged."

"You should advocate for that. Like a human rights campaign at the UN after we outlaw abortion worldwide," Rachel says.

"*Such* a good idea."

We lie back on my bed, full-size with a sunflower-print comforter, matching pillowcases. Rachel's head is at my feet, her feet at my head, Top and Tail, my mother used to call it when she'd tuck us in. We spent countless afternoons like this studying for tests or moaning about being fat virgins, at least until Rachel got thin and I got laid. Rachel served me with divorce papers after I'd had sex first, although I was never sure what the alternative was. One of us was always going to be first. "We're not equal anymore," Rachel said then, her voice icy, her face suddenly neutered of expression. She could do that in seconds, drop her emotional register from ninety to zero.

"Sometimes I think it would just be easier if you were…dead so I wouldn't have to think about how you'll feel every time I do something without you," I said to her at the time.

"You're a bad person," Rachel said. "I hope you get sick and suffer and die of some awful disease."

"I hope so too. Cause then you'll forever live with guilt and have a hideous life."

Rachel expected so much of me, a ravenous desire to be one with me, to live the same life, do everything in lock step. We could make each other miserable which is why the good times felt so exhilarating.

"We whined so much for so long in this room," I say now to Rachel.

"When we thought happy people were shallow, like they couldn't feel things as deeply as we did. Which made us more advanced beings." We nod thoughtfully, the way we'd nodded long ago.

"I'm the happiest I'll ever be, Rache. Maxed out on my Zoloft but really okay. I could go on like this forever and it would be fine. Just right."

"That's so sad," she says. "All that brightness."

"Or it's insurance against not being too sad."

* * *

The summer before high school, Rachel's mom rented a beach shack with chipped concrete steps leading down to a small, half-moon cove. Ancient rock pools bookended the beach and if we were bored enough, we'd wade through the pools in bare feet and stick our big toes into the mouths of swollen sea anemones. When the tide was low the water was pancake smooth, but when the tide came in the waves were jagged and mean and pounding, the water so furious it grabbed most of the beach and emptied the people, their encampments. Rachel knew enough not to swim then, but to stand at the shore, interlock her arm with mine and squeal when the waves smacked our thighs, a gesture that, if you were observing us, could read as adolescent giddiness but was instead Rachel keeping me in place at her side. She knew then that my instinct for self-preservation wasn't like hers, relished her essential role as my protector.

I shook loose one day, swam to where I could no longer stand, where I could do nothing but succumb to the weight of the water. Rachel yelled from the shore, my name over and over, but I drifted below, let the water rush into my ears, over my face. I closed my eyes so that everything notched to slow motion, so that, except for the buzz of my nerves, like a million tiny currents in my ear, I had no defense, couldn't prepare my body for when the wave finally slammed down onto me and I tumbled around inside its spin, Maytagged and disoriented. The way the wave swelled out there, a monster rushing, it terrified and thrilled me, a euphoria so pure, so extreme that anything less would disappoint me forever. Finally, Rachel, as I knew she would, sent the lifeguard out, his bright orange torpedo towing me back to her. We sat together in the foam. Lumps of sand, stiff like a maxi pad, packed in my crotch. A sand crab, its humpback mottled grey, dug down into the sand, buried itself so efficiently, and I felt the weight of Rachel's wet hair on my shoulder.

* * *

Rachel sits up on my bed now and begins to cry. I wonder what's wrong with her. We weren't girls who cried. Rachel, as a point of pride. Me, because I couldn't even if I wanted to.

"You're just going through the motions and I'm the only one who knows it," she says. "I want to go out there and scream it to everyone. *She doesn't love him. It's a transaction.*" She streaks snot over her cheek with the heel of her palm. "He will never know the muck of you."

The truth is that I did love him. But only to a certain point. Between me and my feelings for him, maybe for everyone, hung a scrim, a membrane I could see through, say *I love you too* through, have sex through, but not feel through. It was how I navigated the world. As if my internal pharmacy, understocked, with or without the meds, kept me at a remove. That feeling of standing in place—an opaque nowhere—never able to round the bend to that place where everyone else lived robust, sentient lives.

"And then, at the same time, part of me thinks you're right. Part of me thinks I should be doing this too," Rachel says.

I sit up. Our faces are so close. I notice a stray black hair under her chin, like a witch hat amidst the angelic blonde fuzz, and I have an urge to yank it.

"Well tick tock." I'm being a little mean—there were no men on her horizon, hadn't been for some time—but so is she.

Music from somewhere, maybe the tiki torch house, thumps outside the open window, and a faint breeze moves through the room riffling the organza of the dress ever so slightly. That other party and my dress! Yes! They are openly communing. I slip off the bed to cross the room, grab the dress around the waist and lift it up by its hanger off the door.

* * *

"How do I look?" Rachel asks when I button her into the dress. She thrusts her hips forward and gyrates back and forth, an affront to the dress but one it handles with surprising grace.

"It looks good on you," I say. "You can borrow it when you get married. We'll be featured in Mrs. Magazine: *BFFs marry in same dress*."

"That's a real magazine?"

"It should be," I say. "Everything Mrs."

* * *

The tiki torch house, it's been flirting with me and the dress all evening. So, in a way, it makes perfect sense that we end up here. As we walk up a side entrance, a group of college kids clusters at an open door off the kitchen, the smell of weed like burnt coffee or skunk. Two girls, one in tears, a newer imprint of Rachel and me, are deep in loud conversation. Something about feeling abandoned, mistaking need for love, something you're only entitled to think profound once in your life.

I need a drink not just because it's been a while since my last but because I want to make foggy the facts that I've left my cellphone accidentally, but also on purpose, in my childhood bedroom, at a party thrown in my honor, the honor of my marriage, and that people will be looking for me, at first randomly, and then all of them, all at once. The note I scrawled and left on the pillow of my bed, "Rachel and I on walk—Be back soon!" will only work for so long.

Kids stare as we pass, as Rachel's tail sweeps the ground gathering dirt.

"Are you happy now?" I ask the dress. "Out on the town?"

"Don't talk to me," the dress says in Rachel's helium voice.

"Is this like some bachelorette shit?" a blond kid asks. He looks from me to Rachel to the dress.

"What do you mean?" Rachel asks as she pours from a jug of Smirnoff into a red plastic cup and hands it to me. The kid has a smash face, a snout nose, but also looks like Matt Damon.

"You friends of Brad?" Smash Face Matt Damon asks.

"Cousins," Rachel says. "Where is Bradley?"

"Bradley, hah!" SFMD guffaws like this name never occurred to him before. He points to a group of boys sitting in a ring of beach chairs near a ping pong table, their faces shadowed by the flicker of the torches, like little Klansmen. One wears only a tiara and swim trunks. He stands in the center of their circle jerk and makes dribbling moves with his hands, his pinkies outstretched, stomping one foot, then the other, singing into the shaft of his beer bottle.

The Bradman.

He reminds me of the guy I fucked once at that sober camp, I tell Rachel. She smiles broadly in recognition. "You should have married *him*," Rachel says.

"He died," I say.

"What do you mean died?"

"Like he…stopped breathing?"

"Fuuuuck," Rachel says. She giggles a little self-consciously but then laughs hard and loud. So do I. We can't stop.

"Oh, my fucking god," Brad says when he sees us. "Are you strippers? Like for me?"

"No, Bradley," I say. "Don't be such an idiot."

Rachel wheezes with laughter. I laugh so hard vodka shoots from one nostril, burns my sinuses. Rachel could say *pencil* right now and we'd be on the floor.

* * *

Rachel drives Brad's mom's car, a beige Lexus living room. I ride shotgun, Brad and SFMD in the back. We've agreed to buy them booze because they're eighteen and don't have fake IDs.

"How is that even possible?" I ask Brad when we get in the car.

"It is what it is," Brad says.

"Don't say that Bradley," Rachel says eyeing him in the rearview. "Only stupid people say that."

"Harsh," SFMD says. He passes me a joint over the buttery console and after a hit, I pass it to Rachel.

"You're a vision," I tell Rachel. Moussed in chiffon, smoking a J, holding the wheel of a mom car. She spits smoke, choking on a cough and laughing. And now the boys and I laugh—a whole happy, road-tripping family.

We pull into the Hi Ho Market where we used to bike for Fritos and Mint Milano's. Rachel and I go into the store leaving the kids in the car. As we enter, I link her arm and she puts her head on my shoulder. We walk like that down the liquor aisle until we stop at the refrigerated section, stare into a large glass case of beer. We've been here before—different years, different ages—but Rachel's melancholy, devoid of the usual anger, tells me this is an end of sorts. That in a few hours' time as I make my way down the next aisle, Rachel will slowly recede, and I don't know if it will be because I no longer need her or if she knows she is no longer needed.

"I'm thinking of going off the pill," I say as Rachel reaches for a couple six packs. She thrusts them into my chest and grabs a few more before turning to walk back to the register. I follow, grabbing a bottle of vodka off the shelf. The cashier looks at Rachel's dress, then at me. He congratulates the bride.

I give Rachel a giant kiss on the lips. "We couldn't be happier."

"Vodka's on me," he says. "To the happy lady couple."

"Thank you," we say in unison.

"Actually, I've already gone off," I say as we get back into the car and drive out of the parking lot. The boys are deep in high conversation about Brooklyn and Mahoney, maybe two girls, maybe two venues, hard to tell. I am even, come to think of it, a few days late, already on my way. The thought of potential maternity leave is thrilling. My job, online editor for an NGO, is cutthroat and ridiculously political. Turns out that humanitarians are vicious.

"You can't even take care of yourself, Tessa," I say for her because she still hasn't said anything.

"I think it's good," Rachel says finally.

"No, you don't," I say.

"No, *you* don't," she says.

"Go left," I say at the stop sign. Rachel looks at me. She cocks her head quizzically, like a dog recognizing the mighty word *dinner*, and we begin our descent from the hills.

※ ※ ※

The club we go to is called Break Room. Back in high school it was The Odyssey. It's a low-rise dump, sandwiched between an all-night gas station and a 70's motor inn called *Snooty Fox*. The four of us make our way onto the dance floor, a hot, felty, airless space. EDM blares. I normally hate the assaultive whumping, but tonight it echoes my mood, edgy, anticipatory. Before we left the car, the boys had given us a bump of Special K, an old friend who was with me during those first few years in New York, after I flunked out of college, clubbing every weekend, fucking as many men as I could in bathroom stalls or in cabs at dawn on my way home.

Time stops at last and I'm rounding that corner. Centered and deep inside my body, moving through space, every swing of my arms, flick of my hips. I'm warm, numb all over, smiling at everyone and everything and nothing at all. It's been so long since I've been out dancing and I forget what a good dancer I am, great even. I'm a sensation. I get behind Rachel, grind up on the $3,000 dress, hoist its filthy tail like a canopy. The boys take shelter underneath, and I cast it up over their heads like a parachute. We knead our hips against each other, against the dress. I am full of love for the boys suddenly. Brad has begun to look exceedingly beautiful.

Someone grabs the parachute and I move in front of Rachel now, push my hands upward with open palms. She mirrors me, like we're shoving a carry-on into an overhead, a move we perfected here fifteen years ago. Flight Attendant, we called it. We're both laughing and that feeling of going under, half drowning is where I want to be. Rachel is with me this time, under the water. Then Brad, Brad! He's in my face, he's doing this thing with his pelvis, tipping it forward towards me, knocking his chest against mine. The Bradman! I put my hand on his hip and push into him hard. Now we're both doing it, in and out, together and back. *Watch me, Rachel. Watch.*

Even as I'm leading Brad to the back of the club, to the bathroom, I feel Rachel's eyes on me. Even as I'm pulling him into a stall, pushing him against the closing door, kissing him, I'm being smacked by waves, rolled, and spun. As I grab his shoulders, shimmy a pantleg off my thigh and hoist myself up onto the toilet roll canister putting his dick inside me, waves fall over me like a blanket.

"Where did you go?" Rachel yells into my ear when I appear back on the dance floor.

"Nowhere," I say even though she knows exactly. I can see that some of the silk on the bodice of the dress is torn, sweat rings dilate under the arms. Rachel is drinking as she dances and some of her drink laps over the glass onto the floor, onto the dress. Tears, real ones, are pouring down my cheek now because I'm so happy, because this is the last time I will be this happy. Not tomorrow at my wedding, not even at the birth of my children. I wrap my arms around Rachel's neck, and she encloses me in hers. We sway together amidst the music, the heat, the melee. Soon we will walk out of here. We will have this secret, this secret that we will always carry with us, a gift that binds us, more intimate even than the marriage I am about to embark upon. This is my parting gift to her.

DYANNE STEMPEL *is a writer living in Los Angeles. Her writing has appeared in* Colorado Review, Potomac Review, Valparaiso Fiction Review *and elsewhere. She is a first-place winner of the James Kirkwood Literary Award and is currently at work on a collection of short fiction.*